The Curse of
Madam

James Brumley

The Curse of
Madam

TATE PUBLISHING
AND ENTERPRISES, LLC

Published by Tate Publishing & Enterprises, LLC
127 E. Trade Center Terrace | Mustang, Oklahoma 73064 USA
1.888.361.9473 | www.tatepublishing.com

Tate Publishing is committed to excellence in the publishing industry. The company reflects the philosophy established by the founders, based on Psalm 68:11,
"The Lord gave the word and great was the company of those who published it."

Published in the United States of America

ISBN: 978-1-68118-616-0
1. Fiction / Romance / Gay
2. Fiction / African American / General
15.08.06

I would like to thank Mary Elaine Castle, the coeditor of the *Curse of Madam,* for the hard work she put in working with me. My thanks also goes to Carolyn Barnes for her positive energy and motivation.

Chapter 1

In the small town of Jacksonville, Florida, in 1930, lived Lorene and her seven-year-old son, Ricky Smith. While Ricky was playing with the neighborhood kids down the street from his house, they got into an argument. They then began chasing him with the intent to catch him to cause harm unto him. He ran and he ran, trying to reach his house, where his mother was, screaming, "Momma, Momma!" to the top of his lungs, hoping that his mother would hear him and come to his rescue. He rushed inside the door of the house gasping out of breath, rushing into his mother's bedroom, only to see her giving some strange man oral sex. Once he realized what was going on, he rushed outside, ran to the back of the house, sat in a corner on the side of their white three-bedroom house, and began to cry. She then rose up out of the bed telling the strange man that he had to go, forgetting about the money he owed her for her services. She rushed out of her room and out of the front door barely dressed, calling out for him, saying, "Ricky, baby, where are you?" She did not see him anywhere. She then decided to walk around the house to look for him and found him sitting in a corner on the back of the house, crying his little heart out. She then grabbed him and held him inside her arms, rocking him backward and forward, telling him softly, "Mommy's sorry. Mommy's here." She then picked him up and brought him inside the house. "Tell Mommy what's wrong?"

He said, sniffling, "I was playing with the kids down the street. We got into a argument, and they wanted to beat me up, so I ran!"

"It's okay, son. You are home now. You are safe now, and if dem little f——s lay a hand on you, I want you to pick something up and knock da hell out of 'em, and I bet you they will think twice before messing with you again!" Rick began to smile and felt better from hearing these words spoken to him by his mother.

Lorene had other problems that haunted her other than having sex for money with strange men. She had a very abusive relationship. She was a heavy drinker and loved to stay out all night at the Honky Tonk Club. Lorene's lifestyle kept her from being the best mother she could be for little Rick. Her boyfriend, Earl, would beat her and force sex on her when she did not feel like having it. When she would stay out late hours into the night, she would leave Rick home for hours at a time with Earl. While she would be away, Earl would beat and have his way sexually with little Rick. One night, when Lorene left the house, Rick was taking a bath, sitting inside the tub. Earl was standing outside the bathroom door, peeping in at him while he was taking his bath. He then walked into the bathroom where little Rick was; he stuck his hand inside the water and grabbed little Rick's private area while sticking one of his fingers up little Rick's rectum. Rick began to scream out to Earl, "Stop! Stop! You are hurting me!" He hit Earl on the arm.

"Shut the f——k up!" Earl demanded as his aged rough hand slapped forcefully little Rick's premature cheeks.

Little Rick became silent with tears falling from his eyes. Looking Earl in his eyes, he said, "I'm gonna tell my mommy on you."

Once Earl heard this, he let Rick's privates go and said, "Listen here, you lil' bastard. If you do, I will kill you and ya damn momma!" He grabbed Rick around his neck and held it tightly until Rick's eyes turned red. "Do you hear me?"

Because of little Rick's fear, he said, "Yes."

Earl let his neck go and walked out of the bathroom. From that point on, he was afraid to tell his mother about the things that Earl was doing to him. Sometimes at night, Rick would have nightmares from the result of the things that Earl had done unto him. He would wake up in the middle of the night, screaming to the top of his lungs. One night, when Lorene got in from the Honkey Tonk Club, she heard him screaming. She then rushed into his room where he was sleeping and found out that he was having a nightmare. He was sitting up in the middle of the bed, curled up inside his covers, crying. Lorene asked him, "What's wrong?"

He said in a wrying voice, "The boogie man, Mommy, the boogie man is trying to get me."

Lorene reassured him, "Momma is here, baby. Momma is here," rocking him back and forth in her arms.

Chapter 2

Rick was a very handsome little boy and a very good student. Every afternoon, he would come in and do his homework all by himself.

Other than her party life, Lorene was a pretty good mother. She would have his meals ready every afternoon when he got in from school, and she made sure he was well-dressed for school. She said unto him, "Son, tell me, since you are doing all this homework and everything, tell me what do you want to be when you grow up?"

"I want to become a dancer and then the whole world will then really love me," Rick said, as he rubbed his pencil across his lips.

"I don't know about that dancing stuff, but anything is possible if you dream it and believe it, son. As far as the whole world loving you for it, you got to first love yourself before anybody else can love you. That's what my momma Mamie and momma Georgia told me when I was a little girl. I have found these words to be true."

One afternoon, Rick got inside from school. While he was waiting for the dinner to get ready, he began looking out the window beside the eating table and saw a beautiful butterfly sitting on a flower. It was amazing to him. He thought to himself, *If only, I was a butterfly.* He then said unto his mother, "What would life be like if I was a butterfly?"

Lorene responded, "I do not know, son. I guess your life would be most peaceful."

Little Ricky sat quietly and continued staring outside the window, looking at the butterfly flying around the beautiful flower. One night, when Lorene went out to party at the Honkey Tonk, her boyfriend came in from work and found Rick sitting on the floor, watching television. He grabbed him roughly and pinned him down on the couch.

"Help, help!" Rick began to scream at the top of his voice.

Earl did not stop. He told Rick to be quiet and then hit him. Earl then unbuttoned his pants and forced his penis into Rick's mouth. Rick, contemplating revenge, bit down. Earl screamed, "I am going to kill you, you little f——r!"

Once Rick got free from Earl's hold, he ran to his room and locked himself inside his closet. Lorene came in late that night and saw the bruises on her baby's face. "What happened?"

"Earl did this to me, Mommy."

Lorene went inside the room where Earl was sleeping and began arguing with him about the bruises he put on Rick's face. Rick then got underneath his bed because he was afraid. That night, Lorene told Earl to pack his things and get out of her house. Two weeks later, Lorene got news that Earl got his brains shout out while trying to rob some guys during a dice game. Not long after Earl's death, Lorene started dating another man by the name of Carl at the Honkey Tonk. Carl was no better than her late boyfriend;

he was very abusive. At this point, Lorene and Rick's life was at very hard period, but somehow, they managed to endure. As for Lorene, the struggle was just beginning. A few weeks later, she started to feel pain in her chest. She did not let the pain slow her down; she kept going as if it did not bother her. It began to get worse that next morning; the pain was so sharp it was if pins and needles were holding her to her mattress. That morning, Rick noticed that his mother was really sick. He ran next door, to the neighbor.

Once Mrs. Jones opened her door, she noticed that he panicked. "What's wrong, child?"

"My momma," he said, "she really sick, and she can't get out of bed. She needs to go and see the doctor."

"Well, what we waiting on, child? Let's go!" Mrs. Jones said to Rick.

They rushed over to the house and found Lorene lying on the floor, passed out. Mrs. Jones called the paramedics, and she was transported to the hospital where she stayed for a few weeks. Rick stayed with Mrs. Jones until his mother got out of the hospital.

Ricky was very happy to see his mother come home that afternoon. When she got home, she said to him, "Baby, Mommy is just fine." In the back of his mind, he knew that there was something wrong, but he just did not know what it was.

Chapter 3

From that point on, Lorene knew that her problem was very serious. She had cancer and couldn't bear to tell her little Ricky. She then began to worry about who would take care of Rick if something were to happen to her. She did not have but only one living relative—her aunt Mamie, who was married to a very successful preacher and wealthy businessman who owns an oil company in New Orleans. Lorene decided to call her up to see if she could be of some assistance. Aunt Mamie was the only black woman in the city of New Orleans who owned a black-and-white Bentley car. When Lorene called, Aunt Mamie was extremely excited to hear from her only niece since they hadn't spoken in over ten or fifteen years. Lorene told her aunt Mamie that she needed desperately to come to New Orleans to talk to her about a serious matter concerning her and her son. Aunt Mamie said, "Honey, is it money that you need, baby?"

"No, Aunt Mamie, I just need to come and talk to you face to face."

"Well, child, when would you like to come to this here fine city of New Orleans?"

"As soon as possible."

"Well, child, don't worry yourself about a thang. I'll make arrangement for you and that boy of yours to come her on 'AD train the first thing tomorrow."

When Loraine and Rick boarded the train, Rick was about seven years old at the time. He asked his mother with the look of confusion in his eyes, "Why are we going to see your aunt Mamie?" Then the train pulled forward.

"We are going down there to stay for a couple days. I need to talk to her about some important business."

At that moment, he did not ask any more questions about why they were going on the trip. He just looked outside the window, gazing at the clouds, and became very excited about riding on the train for the first time. When they arrived at the train station in New Orleans, Aunt Mamie and Uncle Pittman were already standing there, excited to see the both of them and to see Rick for the first time. When Rick looked into Aunt Mamie's eyes for the first time, he knew from her smile that they would be friends for a lifetime. She hugged him as if she would be his protector for life. He thought at that moment that he would never want to leave her. When he turned and looked at his mother in the midst of his excitement, he saw peace in her eyes. He knew something was wrong with her, being that they were in that strange city visiting this unknown woman. Whatever the case was, he noticed his mother had a sense of peace that ran across her face. This old lady of whom Rick did not know was a very beautiful light-skinned woman. He instantly said to himself that he wanted to be just like her when he grows up. As they walked through the train station to the car, everyone was just standing and staring at them with big smiles on their faces as if they knew who they were. When they got outside of the train station, there was a man standing by the back door of the car. He then opened the door of the car for them to enter inside; once they all got inside, he then closed the door and began to drive them to Aunt Mamie's house. When they arrived at her house, Rick looked at it as if he had died and went to heaven just by looking at the beauty of it, snow-colored, and the beautiful green grass aliened with a white fence with black horse running around inside it. It appeared as if they had to drive a couple of miles to reach the front door of the house. It was the biggest house little Rick had ever seen in his life. It looked like something Rick had seen in an old slavery book. When they arrived at the front door of the mansion and got out of the car, Joe, the butler, opened the door and let them out. The wind blew across Rick's face, as if it were speaking to his soul, saying you are safe now. When they got inside the house, Aunt Mamie said, "Lorene, your boy is such a petty little boy!"

Uncle Pittman said, "Mamie!"

Momma Mamie said, "Did I say something wrong, hon?"

"A boy is not pretty, he is handsome."

Rick thought he was pretty too. Aunt Mamie then had her maid, named Lady, cook them a big dinner. When they all sat down to the table, Ricky looked at all the food before him. He thought that it had to be Thanksgiving or some major holiday. After dinner that afternoon, Aunt Mamie took him upstairs to the room then she helped put on his pajamas and tucked him into bed. "Ricky, baby, you're a fine young man. You are the finest young man that I have ever seen. I have always wished in the depths of my soul that I could have a little child like you." She began to tell him a story that Momma Bea told her and his great-grandmother Ernestine when they were little girls.

"Once upon a time, there was a little girl who was trapped in a city all by herself. She did not know anybody. Everyone she came in contact with ignored her beauty because it was camouflage by the dirt of the earth. All she wanted was a friend who could see her, not only for her outward beauty, but the natural beauty that lied inside her soul. Every morning after sleeping out on the streets, she would arise and walk around trying to find the friend of her dreams that would give her back the abandoned love that she had lost. Then one day after enduring all the neglect of all those she had come in contact with, in hope of finding the one true friend she longed for, she looked through out the street of New York and still could not find a friend anywhere. That little girl lost hope and sat down on a curve of the street and began to cry. Then it happened. Someone touch her on the shoulder and said, *"Stop crying. There is no need to cry."* It was a little boy dressed in worn-out overalls with holes in the knees of his pants who handed her a piece of apple that he had grab out of a trashcan. The little boy then asked the little girl, *"Why are you so sad?"*

"The little girl said, crying her little heart out, *"My mother has died. She was my best friend. Now I have no friends and no one to love me for my outward beauty and the inward beauty that lies in the depth of my soul, like my mommy loved me before she died. Now she has left me here all alone in this world all by myself."*

"The little boy said, *"You are pretty and nice. Can I love you? I will love you, not only for your outward beauty, I will also love you for the inward beauty that lies inside your soul."*

"At that moment, the little girl stopped crying and wiped the tears that fall from her eyes with the dress tail of her dusty white dress. The both of them loved each other for the rest of their lives. From that day on, she never cried again."

Little Ricky then asked, "Why did your grandmother tell you this story?"

"Baby, anything that your heart desire, if you dream about it and you are persistent and patient, whatever it is that you desire will come and tap you on your shoulder out of the middle of nowhere."

"What was my great-grandmother like?"

"Child, she was sweet as honey. She was one of the most beautiful woman that you ever wanted to see. She was my oldest sister. As a little girl, I wanted to be just like her. All the men in the town wanted to be in her presence. Because of her beauty, most of the women in the town at that time were jealous of her. When she walked inside a room, all the men would focus on her and forget that they had a lady with them. Her name was Ernestine. She loved to go and hang in the Honkey Tonk all night long, with her boyfriend Edward, your great-grandfather, drinking that Moonshine. One night, they went out to the Honkey Tonk to party, while they were out partying and drinking. They ran into Carl's ex-girlfriend Judy who was still in love with Carl and had not got over their breakup. Ernestine and her got into an argument over Carl. Ernestine always had a hot temper and would fight at a drop of a dime. The argument got Ernestine really hot to the point she slapped Judy across her face. Judy then reached inside her purse and streamed out, *"Bitch, you don't f——k up now."* Ernestine told her, *"Bitch, bring it on!"* Judy rush over to Ernestine so quickly. Before she knew it, Judy had cut her throat from ear to ear, leaving her to die in a pool of blood.

"Miss Mabel the town slut came knocking late that night, shortly after the fight took place. Once I heard the beating at the door, in my heart I knew there was something seriously wrong before I got to the door to open it. When I open the door, Miss Mabel was standing there out of breath, holding the bottom of her dress tail in shock.

"She said, *"Girl, where is Mrs. Georgia?"* Momma Georgia was sitting inside the living room, nodding. From hearing all the commotion, it awaken her. She was me and Ernestine mother, your great-grandmother. At that moment, Momma walk up to the door and said unto Mrs. Mabel, *"Child, what's wrong?"*

"She said, *"Ernestine just got killed"*

"Momma's response, *"Child, where is my baby?"* I just stood there speechless, looking into her eyes as she told Momma the story of Ernestine death in shock and disbelief. She went on to say, 'Ernestine got into an argument with Judy, Carl's ex-girlfriend. She cut Ernestine throat ear to ear, leaving her for dead on the floor at the Honkey Tonk."

"Momma then said unto me, *"Child, go and get your Poppa Joe and tell him to get the wagon so we can go and get my baby."* She then cried out in a loud voice, saying, *"Lord, help my soul. Please don't let my baby be gone."*

"I was seventeen years old at the time. I ran as fast as I could screaming to the top of my lungs, calling my father's name, hoping he might hear me. Once I made it to the back of the house where he was sleeping, I said unto him, *"Poppa wake up, wake up."*

"He said, *"Girl, what's wrong?"*

"I then went on to tell him, "Momma Georgia said get the wagon. Ernestine has just got killed."

"Poppa Joe got up and got the mules together for the wagon and drove us down to the Honkey Tonk where Ernestine was lying dead in the middle of the floor of that devil's workshop. When we walked into the doors of the Honkey Tonk, we saw Ernestine lying in the middle of the floor in a pool of her own blood with her throat cut from ear to ear. When Momma saw her, she passed out as if the good Lord above had taken her breath away into Poppa Joe's arm. He was also broken up with tears falling from the wells of his eyes. At that moment, seeing my sister lying there in all of that blood, I rushed over to her, barely seeing from the tears that fell from my eyes. With all the strength in me, I picked her head up out of the blood that fell from her neck and held her close to the bosom of my chest, leaving blood all over the white gown I had on. At that moment, all I could say aloud, *"Oh, my sister is gone! What will I do now, O God, O God? What will I do now that you have taken her far from my heart?"* I then began to cry like I had never cried before. At that moment, I felt like I could have died because of the hurt that pierced my soul. Poppa Joe was a very big and robust man. He then walked over and picked Ernestine up from the floor and put her in the back of the wagon taking her to the town's funeral home to get her dressed for her homegoing. The day of the funeral, we were all sitting inside the living room area, viewing Ernestine's remains, waiting for the time to go the funeral when I heard a knock at the door. In my mind, I thought that it was some more of Momma's friends. To my surprise, it was the county sheriff.

"He asked me, *"Where Momma Georgia?"*

"At the time, Momma was sitting inside the living area in her favorite chair with all her friends. At that time, she was eighty-two years old. He then asked if he could speak to her for a moment.

"I then said, *"Right this way."* He then followed me into the room where Momma Georgia and Momma Bea were sitting. Once he entered the room, where everyone was waiting with Momma Georgia, he took off his hat and said good afternoon to everyone. He then walked closer to Momma Georgia and Momma Bea and said, *"How are you doing? I am sorry about what happen too Ernestine."*

"Momma Georgia looks up at him with a smile on her face. *"Thank you, son. It is good to see you."* She was his nanny; he practically grew up with Ernestine ever since he was a child.

"He went on to say unto her, *"She was just like a sister to me."* Tears began to fall from his eyes as he spoke these words unto her. *"I don't want to keep you long. I have come to let you know that I have the lady who murdered your daughter in jail."*

"At that moment, I walked over to the chair where Momma was sitting and put my hand on her shoulder. Momma then raised her head and said unto the sheriff, *"Son, let that child go so she can go home and take care of her children for vengeances is not mines, but the Lord's."*

"He then said, *"Are you sure, Momma Georgia?"*

"She said, *"Yeah, son, I am sure."*

"I then helped her out of her chair and walked her to the front door so we could go and bury Ernestine, leaving the sheriff standing speechless from the words in which Momma spoke. From hearing the words she spoke unto the sheriff, the room became silent and surprised with the spirit that flowed inside her heart.

"Your grandmother Irene was about seven months old at the time, when her mother Ernestine got killed. Momma Georgia and I raised her from that point on. She grew up as if she was my little daughter. She grew up to be the most beautiful young lady you ever wanted to see. Unfortunately, her sinful desires and her beauty began to drain the life of God out of her soul. You know child you have that same beauty that your grandmother Irene had. You know, son, I see that same smile in your eyes, child, that I saw in hers many years ago. When I went away to college, I left Irene with Momma to look after her. Of course, she lived a little on the wild side like her mother Ernestine. Every other weekend, Momma would call me to let me know how Irene would go to those Godforsaken places with that wild man of hers your grandfather Henry, get her self lockup in jail. Momma Georgia would always bail her out of jail many times. One night, her and Henry were driving home from the Honky Tonk filled with that devil's drink and got them killed in a car wreck. At the time, she had your mother Loraine. She was just a baby. The funniest thing happened. Ernestine died the same day, and the same age that Irene did, her baby your mother was the same age that she was when her mother got killed."

Little Rick asked Momma Mamie, "Why is it that they died so young and you did not?"

Momma Mamie said unto him, "Baby honey child, I really do not know. I believe that the voodoo slave ghost paid them a visit and cause the curse of the madam to fall on their heads, a curse that was passed down the seed of Momma Bulla robbing the life of their soul."

He then asked her, "Aunt Mamie, what is the curse?"

"Hush, child, you are too young to worry about that now. When you get a little bit older, I will tell you more about it, and maybe one day, I will tell you how to escape it yourself."

"How is it that you survived it?"

"Honey baby child, it was nobody but God and my husband that allowed me to barley make it through the clutches of the curse, however it robbed me of my babies, of my womb, leaving me barren. That's the reason I am so glad that you are here, child, so that the seed of the black madam may live on."

"When I grow up, I wanted to be just like you, Aunt Mamie."

"Son, just grow up and be a man. Just be a man"—she rubbed his face gently—"child, your old Mamie love you." There was a smile of hope in her eyes as she looked upon his face.

"I love you too, Aunt Mamie."

"Just call me Momma Mamie, child. Now go to sleep. You have a long day ahead of you tomorrow." She then kissed him on his forehead and tucked him in for the night.

As she walked toward the door and opened it to leave the room, Rick then said unto her, "Momma Mamie, I hope that the curse of madam do not ever take you."

"Baby honey child, as long as I keep mine hand in God's hand, that old curse can never do me no harm, child." She then smiled, and he did too.

Chapter 4

The next morning when Rick awoke, Lady, the maid, had breakfast by his bedside. It was the first time he had ever had anyone bring him breakfast in bed. While he was eating breakfast, Momma Mamie and Lorene were downstairs eating breakfast in the dining quarters. While they were eating, Momma Mamie said, "Child, tell me what it is that trouble your soul. I have not heard from you in over fifteen years. I have called many times, but the phone number that I have for you, I could not reach you at it. Baby honey child, all my life, my heart has been broken by the ones that I hold close to my heart because of that curse." She then rose out of her seat and walked over to the window with tears in her eyes and said unto Lorene, "When Momma Georgia was on her deathbed, she asks of you, saying, *"Where is our darling Lorene? We have not heard from her in a long time, child. You reckon the curse of the madam has taken her far from our hearts, child."* I then said unto her, *"No, Momma. She's somewhere..."* hoping in my heart you were still alive somewhere.

"Momma then said unto me, *"I hope that, that child didn't go and be hardheaded like Ernestine and Erlene running after of those loose men and getting her heart hurt, hon. She's all we got that will supersede the legacy of Momma Bea. Mamie, I want you, with your beautiful self, to go and try to find that child and bring her to me. I just want to look upon her face and behold her beauty once more."*

"I told my Momma on that Sunday afternoon, *"Don't you go on talking about breaking my heart too, Momma. I just want to see her one more time before I depart from this life unto the next."* At that moment, I began to cry, I can't take any more pain. *"Momma, you are just breaking my heart into pieces."*

"Momma said unto me, *"Hush, child, now when the Lord gets ready for you, child, it ain't no stopping him from doing his will. Baby, when he do call my name, hon, I am ready to go, because these old eyes of mine have seen enough, baby. I'm one hundred and fifteen years old. It's pass time for me to go. Baby honey child, I'm tired of fighting year after year with the curse that witch slave robbing me of all of them that I love. I am tired Mamie. You know baby, you are the strongest one of those girls, and the Lord has protected your head from the hidden curse of Momma Bulla and Momma Bea. Be strong, baby, for our darling Lorene, because Momma Georgia is going to have to say good-bye to this old world, and when the good Lord take me, baby, the seed of the madam will be left in your hands so that the black madam can continue to live on. Above all else, baby, find our Lorene and makes sure that she is a lady. You know, child, you have to protect that child and her seed because that voodoo slavery is going to come and pay you a visit one day, child. I want you to know, as long as you keep your hand in God's hands, the will protect you like he did me and my momma from the curse of the abuse voodoo slave. May God rest its soul. It has been my prayer that God let rest fall on her soul so that the black madam may have peace one of these days."* After speaking these things unto me, she passed away, holding my hand."

Then Momma Mamie cried as she looked out the window of the dining room. She then turned and looked at Lorene and said, "I looked and looked for you high and low, child. Once I realized I couldn't find you so that you could come to Momma's funeral, it broke my heart into pieces. When I buried Momma, seeing those men throw the dirt of the earth in her face, I felt as if I was in this world all by myself." Then Momma Mamie wiped her tears with a white handkerchief.

Lorene began to cry, walked over to the other side of the table where she was sitting, patted her on her back, and said unto Momma Mamie, "Momma, I'm so sorry." Lorene then knelt down on the floor next to her and grabbed her hand. "Aunt Mamie, the reason that I didn't call or write, I didn't want to bother you with my problems. My life was not right. I had turned my face from the bosom of God for the sins of this world. I began to drink and prostitute my body for money so that I could provide for my child."

Aunt Mamie then said, "Why, child, you don't have to want for nothing. Look around you, child, the Lord has blessed me with so much earthly possessions. That, child, I give and I give so much away unto the point I can't give it away. Baby, my god, you are my only living relative. My god, child, you didn't have to go to the streets of the devil and beg for money by selling your body, child, going against the good Lord of heaven. Hon, that just breaks my heart into pieces. Why? Lorene, please just tell me why?

"I didn't want to be a burden. I just wanted to stand on my own two feet and provide for my child on my own." She walked back over to her chair and sat down. "It seemed, the harder I tried to be a good mother like you and Momma Georgia, it appeared that the good Lord above just didn't give me enough strength to do so."

Momma Mamie stood up and walked over to where she was sitting. She then held her hand and said unto her in a low, mellow tone, "I know, child, I know. Now, child, tell me what is it that has been troubling you that has brought you too see your Aunt Mamie."

Lorene stood up in front her seat, walked over to the windows of the dining quarters, and looked over the beautiful flowers that were spread out over the lawn. "I came to tell you that a doctor back home examined me. Momma, I found out that I am dying of breast cancer, and I don't know what I am going to do. I have no one to turn to but you. If something were to happen to me, I don't have anyone to look after my baby." She then broke down crying even more.

Momma Mamie walked over to her with a broken heart and touched her, patting her on her shoulder, catching hold of the window seal. "Everything, my child, will be fine." She then called out for her butler, saying, "Baby honey child, will you take the madam to her resting quarters?"

As Lorene and Joe walked through the double glass doors of the dining quarters, she held tightly to his arm. He asked her, "Must I call Reverend Pittman?"

"No, child, just take me to my resting quarters."

Momma Mamie then softly said unto him, stopping momentarily, "Find my baby the finest doctor that New Orleans has to offer that can help her with the burden that troubles her soul."

Chapter 5

The next morning, the doctor arrived to examine Lorene. Uncle Pittman and Momma Mamie were waiting in the living quarters. Momma Mamie sat in one of the high chairs crying, holding a tissue in her hand, wiping the tears that fell from her eyes. Uncle Pittman was standing right beside her for support, praying to the good Lord up above. That morning, little Rick was sent out with the ranch hand to practice horseback riding. He was so excited to learn how to ride a horse, by it being he had never rode one before. In the meantime, the doctor examined his mother. He did not know anything about her doctor's visit. Once the doctor finished the examination, he then began walking down the stairway. Joe was standing at the end of the stairway, waiting for him to come down with the results.

Once he reached the end of the stairway, he said unto him, "I have finished my examine."

Joe then said, "Right this way."

They walked over to the living quarters where the Pittmans were waiting. When he approached the doors of the living quarters, he then told the doctor to please wait so he could alert them that the examination was finished. He then knocked on the door.

Mr. Pittman said, "Enter."

Joe opened the doors to the room where they were sitting. "Reverend Pittman and Madam Mamie, the examination is finished. The doctor is ready to speak with the both of you."

Reverend Pittman then said, "Let him in."

The doctor then came in. "I'm sorry, madam and sir. Lorene has waited too late to be cured of her sickness. It's just a matter of time before it takes her. The cancer has spread all over her body. There is nothing I can do for her that would stop it. I gave her some pain medication to relieve her of the pain that disturbs her body that she might rest easily until her time comes."

He then handed Reverend Pittman a drug prescription. At that moment, Momma Mamie began to cry even more, saying in a loud but gentle voice, "Oh, my baby, the seed of Momma Bea is now being pulled far away from my heart."

She then asked her husband to hold her hand and lead her to the room so she can lie down for a moment. When Rick returned from riding horses, he noticed Momma Mamie was not happy and cheerful as she normally is. She then said to him, "Go, child, to the room where your mother is laying down, resting." Immediately, he knew that something was wrong, and the excitement that he had before he entered inside the mansion was now gone. He began to walk up the stairs, slowly wondering in his mind if his mother was okay. Once he entered into the room where she was resting, he saw her lying in the bed, covered with white covers sleeping. Once he walking closer to her bed of passing, she opened her eyes. Once she awoke and saw that he was in the room, she tried to sit up, but the weakness of her body would not allow her to do so.

She then said unto him, "Come here, baby, and sit down on the bed next to mommy." Momma Mamie then turned and left the room, closing the door behind her as she exited.

Lorene then said to Rick, patting the bed, "Sit here next me." Once he got on the bed, Lorene said unto him, "Mommy is sick. I will be leaving, and I will be gone for a long time. I need for you to stay here with your Momma Mamie and Uncle Pittman to look after you while I am gone."

Rick had tears in his eyes. "Momma, where are you going? Why can't I go along with you?"

"Baby, where momma is going, you can't go with me, because where I'm going, it's not your time yet. I'm going to a place far beyond the blue sky to see God, to talk him about all my problems."

"Mommy, why won't he let me come with you?" There were tears falling from his eyes. "Why won't he let me come too?"

"Because he wants you to stay and take care of your Aunt Mamie. I'm going home to see Momma Irene, Momma Bea, Momma Ernestine, and Momma Georgia.

"Why, Mommy? Why, Mommy?

"That's just the way God wants it. One day he will let you come to be with me."

Rick then began to cry, even more looking into his mother's teary eyes.

Rising up from her bed of affliction, she then said, "Son, be strong. Grow up and be a fine young man and make your momma proud. And don't give your Aunt Mamie and Uncle Pittman a hard time."

"Okay, Momma."

"Now, baby, get down from the bed and go tell your Aunt Mamie to come here. I need to talk too her." Rick got down from the bed, snuffling and crying from the brokenness that lay in the midst of his heart. As he walked toward the door, Lorene said unto him, "Rick, baby."

Rick then turned around, "Yes, Mommy?"

She then asked him the question that Momma Georgia asked her when she was a little girl. "Will you, baby, give me a madam that will supersede the legacy of Momma Bea?"

From hearing the words that was spoken by his mother, he didn't know in actuality what it was that she was asking of him. He responded, with many tears falling from the pit of his eyes, "Yes, Momma, I'll give you a madam that would supersede the legacy of Momma Bea."

Lorene then smiled like she had never before as he turned and walked out of the room. It was as if her pain and misery had left her for a moment. Later, Momma Mamie came into the room, where she was laying in much pain.

Momma Mamie said unto her, "Child, how are you feeling?"

Lorene then said, "Momma, I am hurting all over, and I am worried about my baby. I am sorry, Aunt Mamie, that I have broken your heart like this.

Mamie responded, "Oh, child, my evening star, God knows best, honey." Tears filled the wells of her eyes.

"I didn't want to come here on you like this and die. I just didn't have anyone else to turn to."

"Honey, what better place for you to come and lay down your burdens than here at home where you belong. Baby honey child, this home here is your home. The reason I bought this house, because it was once Momma Bea's house."

"How could Momma Bea afford a house like this during her time in history?"

"Momma Bulla and Momma Bea received this house in a will from father John Edward Armstrong, their slave owner who was your great-great-grandfather. Because of the love he had for Momma Bulla and Momma Bea, he left this plantation to her in his will. Before Momma Georgia died, she told me the dreams that her mother had for the seeds of the black madam. Momma Bulla's dream was that the seed of black madam be a lady of class and style like that of the white madam. Because of her entrapped chains of slavery, she could not fulfill that dream. Her desire was that the seed of the black madam live inside this very house left to her by her father. You and I and that boy of yours, we are that seed. Before Momma died, she told me about this house and how she was unable to keep up the taxes on it. At that time, she told me that it was being put back on the market to be sold. I knew that she didn't want to lose the house. It was the only thing she had left that her mother gave her. I thank the good Lord above for blessing me with my darling husband, Pittman. He had enough money to purchase it for me.

"Momma Bulla was a beautiful black woman during the mid 1800s. She was a house Negro in this very house. During the time she was working in the house, Master Armstrong found favor with her. He also taught her how to read and write. They later fell in love with one another. To this union, Momma Bulla became pregnant with Momma Bea. The other house slaves found out about her pregnancy and began talking about her white child.

Madam Armstrong later found out that she was pregnant with Master Armstrong's child. She told him to put her out of the house into the fields with the other slaves. That was not enough for Madam Armstrong. She became very angry with Momma Bulla. Because of the infidelity that lied between her and Poppa Armstrong, thinking in her mind that by it being that she was placed back into the fields with the other field niggars. The love between them would stop, however it didn't. Once Momma Bea was born, Madam Armstrong became furious. Because of the rage that lied within her soul, one night, while Poppa Armstrong was sleeping, she snuck out of the bed and walked silently down the stairway into the kitchen. She opened the kitchen drawer and got a butcher knife in the middle of the night. She then walked from the house into the fields wearing a snow white-colored gown into the hut where Momma Bulla and her Negro child were sleeping. She then cut Momma Bulla's throat from ear to ear, with the intent to inflict the blade of death into the Negro child as well. Suddenly, Poppa Armstrong was awakened by one of the house Negro slaves named Nappy who was Momma Bulla's best friend, who saw Lady Armstrong sneaking out walking toward the fields with a butcher knife in her hand. She knew in the back of her mind that Madam Armstrong's intent was to kill Momma Bulla. She immediately rushed upstairs to awake Poppa Armstrong to tell him that she had seen her walking out toward the fields with a knife in her hand. From hearing these words, he jumped up from his bed and threw on his slippers and robe on, rushing down the stairs and out of the front door, running with all of his might, hoping that he would get to the hut in the nick of time, to stop his wife before she killed the love of his life. Once he made it to the front door of the huts, he rushed inside to find her with the knife in her hand dripping with blood with the intent to kill his Negro child. He then rushed over to her and stopped her in the nick of time, catching her hand before she inflicted it into the baby. He then took the knife out her hand, saying, *"My god, what have you done, Doris? My god, what have you done!"* He picked up the crying child and held her close to his chest.

"She then stood there, crying aloud, *Is this what you love? Is this what you love. this dam niggar?"* falling to her knees, crying aloud. He then looked at the love of his life lying in her bed covered in blood. He then walked over to where Momma Bulla was laying and fell down on his knees, crying, saying unto her dead corpses, *"My god, Bulla, what have she done unto you,"* holding their baby, crying inside his arm. From that point on, Poppa Armstrong gets up from her bedside and walked out of the hut, leaving Doris, his wife, on the floor, crying. Poppa Armstrong brought Mama Bea inside the plantation and raised her as if she was a white madam with her two sisters Mary and Bertha and their brother little Jimmy. Momma Bea was five years old at the time. When Poppa Armstrong died, he left a large amount of money and the plantation to Momma Bea too. The other children, he left something but not as much as he left Momma Bea. After his death, Lady Armstrong made life really hard for her.

"When it came time for the reading of the will of his estate, Lady Armstrong did not want her to know anything about the will, so she kept it hidden from her and persuaded her children to keep it a secret as well. After the reading of the will, she was even more disappointed to find that Poppa Armstrong had left the plantation to Momma Bea. Once

Momma Bea grow up to be a teenager, Lady Armstrong told her that she had to leave with the belief that she had no right to be on the plantation now that her father was dead. Knowing in her heart that Poppa Armstrong pretty much left everything to her in his will. She gave her two hundred dollars and had the slave driver to take her to the train with a train ticket for Atlanta, Georgia. At that moment she did not know what she was going to do from that point on. She left New Orleans in 1875, not knowing of her inheritance in which her father left her. Once she made it to her destination, she found a job working as a nanny for a white family the Johnsons. During her time working for them, she managed to save a enough money to go to nursing school, to become a nurse. She later met and married a man by the name of Paul Milton who was a blacksmith. He owned his own business. To this union, she had a little girl named Georgia. Once I graduated from college, I brought this house back from the tax office so that the black madam may have it so that she could keep the dream of Momma Bulla alive."

Lorene then said, "I remember when I was a little girl, Momma Georgia would ask me the question, 'Baby honey child, will you give me a madam that would supersede the legacy of Momma Bea?' I then responded, 'Yes, Momma, I'll give you a madam that will supersede the legacy of Momma Bea.' I never knew what she meant by that."

Momma Mamie then said, "I know, baby, when I was a little girl, her and Momma Bea asked me and Ernestine that same question. At the time, I did not know what it meant until Momma Georgia told me the history of the black madam."

Lorene then asked Momma Mamie, "What is the history of the black madam?"

Momma Mamie then said, "When Momma Bea was a little girl, Momma Bulla would dance around the slave hut in a white dress that Poppa Armstrong had bought her as if she was like that of a white woman. Her and Momma Bea would sit inside the hut and have tea parties with the ten cups that the slaves were given to drink out of like that white madam would do with her daughters. She would always ask Momma Bea, 'Baby honey child, will you give me a madam that will supersede the legacy of the black madam so that the black madam may live?' Momma Bea said to her, 'Yes, momma, I will give you a madam that will supersede the legacy of the black madam.' At that moment, Momma Bulla smiled and said, 'That's my little lady. From that point on, this saying was passed down through the generation of the black madam to assure that the seed of the black madam would live on."

After Momma Mamie finished telling the history of the madam, she saw that Lorene's pain was wearing down on her. "Now, child, get you some rest." Early the next morning, Momma Mamie went into Lorene's room to check on her. She tried to wake her up, but she would not wake up. Momma Mamie found out that she died in her sleep. Once she realized this, she cried out for Uncle Pittman. She then began to cry, screaming out, "My baby is gone."

Once Uncle Pittman heard her scream, he rushed up the stairs into the room where Lorene's corpse was lying. Momma Mamie was hovered over it, crying. She then looked up at him and said, "My baby is gone. Who will carry out the legacy of Momma Bea now?"

She then began to cry even more. At that moment, he walked over and grabbed her and held her in his arms. They did not know that little Rick was sitting outside the door of the room with his head between his knees, crying. Once Momma Mamie heard him crying outside the door of the room, she went out the room where he was sitting and knelt down close to him and put her hands around him. He then raised his head. "Is my mommy gone to see God now?"

"Yes, child, she has gone to meet God," Momma Mamie said, with tears running down her face. She then grabbed him and held him close to her bossom.

After the funeral service, all of Momma Mamie's friends came over to the house. Little Rick did not say much after the services; he just sat on the couch and said nothing to anyone. Later on that night, as he was getting ready for bed, Momma Mamie came and brought him some cookies and milk. She asked him as she sat the cookies on the nightstand, "How are you feeling?

He then said, "Who's going to be my mommy now, Aunt Mamie, now that my Mommy has gone to see God?"

Mommy Mamie said, "I am going to be your mommy now. Your mommy left you for me to take care of you."

He then grabbed her and gave her a big hug. "I promise I won't hurt you or bring you any trouble."

She then smiled and said, "I know, child, I know. You know, baby, you are a very handsome young man. The girls are going to go crazy over you." She rubbed her fingers through his curly head of hair. "Go to sleep and rest now for we have a long day ahead of us tomorrow. Your old Momma Mamie and your Uncle Earl going to take you shopping for some more school clothes. I cannot have my new son going out looking any kind of way." She then kissed him on his forehead. "I am so glad your mother decided to bring you home to me. I always wanted to have a little child like you. You know, baby, you and I are going to have a great time together."

Chapter 6

The next morning when they awoke, Momma Mamie and Uncle Pittman took Ricky out for a day of shopping. While they were out and about, sitting down eating lunch, Uncle Pittman asked him, "Son, what kind of sports do you like playing?"

Rick said, "I never really played any sport. I love playing Hopscotch back at home. I really would like to learn how to play tennis."

Momma Mamie and Uncle Pittman looked at each other as if they were surprised, as if they were saying to themselves, *What kind of boy is this who likes to play hopscotch and tennis?* The next week, they enrolled him into his first tennis lesson. He was a very fast learner; his coach was impressed with his ability in playing the game. As he grew, he became the team champion by his ninth grade in high school. He was not only good in the sport of tennis, he also had a very good singing voice like that of a little angel. He sang so well that the adult choir would let him sing as lead singer on some Sundays. Momma Mamie thought she would have to make him get up to sing because of his shyness, but once he got started, he was dynamic. Little Rick was not the only highlight of Sunday morning; service people would come for all parts of the city to hear Pastor Pittman preach his dynamic sermons. Being a very shy child, Rick mainly stayed to himself during his high school years. He was a very attractive young man. Many of the high school girls liked him, but he would just ignore them. One day when Rick came from school, Momma Mamie was setting out tulips in the back lawn. Rick rushed into house and put his book bags and his tennis bag on the table. He called out for Momma Mamie and noticed she was not in the house. He decided to walk outside and found her working in her flower garden. Once she heard him calling, she then said unto him, "Over her, my son." Once he made it to the garden where she was sitting, she said, "How was your day, son?" as he kissed her on the cheek.

"I had a great day."

"Boy, when are you going to bring one of them fine high school girls over to the house? As handsome as you are, I just know they are all over you."

"I really don't have time for any girls. I have too much homework and studying I have to do. Besides, I spend most of my spare time playing tennis. I guess I just have not ran into the right one yet.

"You know the Bible says a man that finds a good woman finds a good thing."

"I know, Momma. One day I will find the right one."

"Don't let the hair on your head turn gray before you do so. Have you been thinking about whom you will be taking to that high school dance? It will be coming up in a few weeks."

"I haven't really thought much about it."

"Son, where is your mind? You don't want to be the only boy at that dance without a date. I want you to find you a young girl to go to that dance with you. Do you hear me, child? And stop being so shy."

"Okay, Momma, I will."

"I hope so, baby, so I can take you and buy you a nice suit to wear."

One afternoon after school, Rick was out at the tennis court practicing with one of his teammates for a game that they had coming up in a few weeks. He noticed a very beautiful light-skinned girl, dressed in a white tennis dress staring at him while he was practicing. She noticed that he was a very great player. Once he finished playing, she picked up her tennis bag and put it on her shoulder then walked over to him to introduce herself. Rick at the time had sat down to cool off when she approached him. She walked up to him and shook his hand. "Hi, my name is Tamarra Augustine."

He then looked up and shook her hand. "My name is Rick Smith. It is a pleasure to meet you."

"While you were playing out there on the court, I noticed that you are a very great tennis player."

"I do pretty good."

"No, you are really good."

"Thank you."

"Maybe we will get an opportunity to play one another sometime after school?"

"That sounds like a great idea, just let me know when."

"How about tomorrow after school?"

"That will be great. I don't have anything planned."

"I guest I will see you on the tennis court tomorrow?"

"Great, I will see you tomorrow. I hope you have on your playing shoes.

She then said, "Oh, I will and smile."

The next day after school, Rick and Tamarra met on the tennis court. They first warmed up by doing a light excise. Once they started to play, Rick was playing easy, not knowing that she was an excellent player herself. Once he realized that Tamarra was no amateur, he began playing hard. She was very hard for him to beat; he managed to beat her. After their game was over, she was very impressed by Rick's playing skills.

Rick said, "Great game. Why didn't you tell me that you play as good as you did?"

"You never asked. Hmmm. Are you going to the high school dance that is coming up?"

"I haven't really just thought about it much. If I don't find someone to go with me soon, my mother is going to kill me. Do you have a date yet?

"No, a lot of boys has been asking me to go with them, but I don't want to go with them."

"Well, would you be willing to go with me?"

"I would love to."

"That's great. You don't know how much this means to me." He was so happy he dropped his tennis racket, trying to pick up his bags, while he was doing so, Tamarra was smiling at him. He could not wait to tell his Aunt Mamie. He then asked her, "Would you like to come over to my house and hang out with me and meet my Momma Mamie after school tomorrow?"

"I would love to, but I have to asked my mother and father first."

"I will let Momma Mamie know that you might come over."

She then said, "I will let you know tomorrow at school."

When he got home that afternoon from school, he was real excited about meeting Tamarra and the fact that she agreed to go to the high school dance with him. He rushed through the door, calling out Momma Mamie's name. He found her studying the Bible.

He said, "Momma, guess what! I found a date to go with me to the high school dance."

"That's great, son. Who is this girl that you have chosen? Does she carry herself like a lady?"

"Yes, she is really nice. We played tennis together today and I asked her if she would come to the dance with me and she said yes! I asked her to come over tomorrow after school and hang out with me and meet you if that's *okay* with you and Uncle Pittman."

"That's great, son. You will have to ask Pittman if it will be okay. If he says yes, we will look forward to meeting your new friend. In the meantime, I will be looking for you a new suit and some new shoes."

That afternoon at dinner, Rick said to his Uncle Pittman, "Uncle Pittman, I met a really nice girl the other day, and we played tennis together. She even asked me to go to the high school dance with her."

Reverend Pittman said, "That's great, son. Aren't you suppose to ask her to go out to the dance with you?"

"Yes, sir. Sorry, Uncle Pittmam, I mean that I ask her to come along with me."

Momma Mamie said, "Leave the boy alone. Who says a girl can't ask a boy to go out?"

Rick then said unto Reverend Pittman, "I was wandering if she could come over tomorrow after school to hangout with me and meet you and Momma Mamie."

Reverend Pittman said, "If it okay with Mamie, it will be just fine with me."

Rick's excitement rushed through his veins. "May I be excused, Momma Mamie?"

"You may."

The next day, Tamarra saw Rick in the hallway. He was still excited about meeting her. She walked up to him with a smile on her face because her father allowed her so easily to come over to Rick's house. He noticed the look she had on her face. "What did he say? Did he say yes?"

She said, "Yes! Once he found out who your mother was, they practically pushed me out the door this morning so that I could come and hang out with you. My father and mother are pretty strict when it comes to boys. Because of who your mother is, they did not have any problem with me coming over to your house. It's crazy, but I will see you after school."

After school on that afternoon, Momma Mamie, as usual, sent their driver to the school, to pick up Rick and Tamarra, in her two-tone black-and-white Bentley. When they walked out of the school doors, Joe was standing outside of the car by the back door, on the passenger side, with the door opened for them to enter in. When they arrived at the mansion, Tamarra was amazed with the beauty of the house and the landscape that surrounded it.

She said to Rick, "You have a beautiful house."

He said, "Thank you, but it not my house, it Momma Mamie and my Uncle Pittman house."

Once they drove up to the front door of the mansion, Uncle Pittman and Momma Mamie were waiting on their arrival. Once they entered inside the house, Pussy Wussy, Momma Mamie's dog, ran up, began to sniff Tamarra, and began to wag her tail. When Momma Mamie met her, she liked her because of the way she carried herself with style and class. They went inside the living quarts and sat down to talk.

Momma Mamie said, "So tell me a little about yourself."

Tamarra said, "Well, I just moved her from New York City with my mother and father.

"What caused your parents to move to New Orleans?"

"My father moved here to work as an accountant for this major oil company called A&B oil company."

Momma Mamie and Uncle Pittman looked at each other with very surprised looks on their faces. They knew that it was their company that she had spoken of.

Momma Mamie then asked, "What is your father name?"

"His name is Kenneth Jones."

Momma Mamie said, "Oh."

Tamarra said, "Do you know him?"

Momma Mamie said, "I'm afraid not, darling." Then she said unto Rick, "Why don't you take your new friend around the mansion and show here around? Dinner will be ready in a couple of hours."

He then stood from his seat and kissed her on the cheek. "Okay, Momma." He then continued, "Come on, Tamarra, let me show you around the place before dinner."

As Tamarra and Rick walked through the lawn of the mansion, Tamarra said, "Your mother and your father are really rich."

"They are not really my mother and father. They are my aunt and uncle. When I was a little kid, my mother and me lived in Jacksonville, Florida. When my mother got sick and knew she was dying, she decided to bring me here to stay with Momma Mamie so she could take care of me."

"I am sorry. I did not know."

"That's okay. I am really happy that she brought me here. They treat me like I am their real son."

When dinner was ready, Joe came out to announce that dinner was now being served. Once they entered the house, Momma Mamie and Uncle Pittman were inside the living quarters, waiting. Once Rick and Tamarra got inside, they all entered inside the dining quarters to be seated, where dinner was served.

While eating dinner, Momma Mamie said unto Tamarra, "Rick tells me that you have agreed to go with him to the high school dance as his date."

She said, "Yes, I did. I think that he is a very nice gentleman."

Momma Mamie said, "Have you prepared yourself for the event?"

"Not yet. Me and my mother are going shopping this weekend for the dress that I will be wearing to the dance."

Momma Mamie said, "That's great. I believe me and Rick will shopping for him something to wear. You can come if you like. We might just find you something too."

"I would love to, if it all right with Ricky."

Rick responded, "I would love for you too come along with us!"

Uncle Pittman said, "I shall come along with you Mamie. We will make a family outing of it."

Momma Mamie said, "It is final, Tamarra, ask your parents if it would be okay if you can go shopping with us on Friday." She then turned unto Uncle Pittman, "My lord, is this day, okay with you?"

Uncle Pittman said, "That day will be fine with me. I just have to finish up some paperwork at the office and talk to my CEO. Once I am finish with all of that, I should be done no later than three o'clock that afternoon. I figure we should go shopping after the children get out of school."

Momma Mamie said, "That's a great idea. I will have the driver to pick you children up from school and meet me and the reverend back here at the house."

Tamarra and Rick smiled at each other because of their excitement of going shopping together. After dinner, Momma Mamie had the driver take Tamarra home. Momma Mamie was really impressed with Tamarra—lady like character. The night of the dance, Ricky was dressed really nice. His hair was curly and slicked back; on his head, he had on a black suit. Before he left the house, Momma Mamie told him to "please remember to always open and close the door for your lady friend." She also told him that she was proud of him. She kissed him on the forehead and told him to go and have a great time and not to forget to carry himself like a gentleman.

Once the driver brought the car around, Rick entered inside and headed off to the dance. Momma Mamie and Uncle Pittman were standing on the front porch, waving good-bye to him. When Rick arrived at Tamarra's house, the driver got out and opened the door for him. He got out of the car, walked to the front door of her house, and knocked. Her father answered the door.

Rick said, "Is Tamarra ready?"

Her father smiled. "Not yet, son. Please come in and have a seat."

When he walked inside, he had the corsage in his hand that Momma Mamie and purchased for him to give to her.

Tamarra's father then took a seat with him. "Tamarra tells me that you're a very great tennis player."

He then says, "She's pretty good herself."

At that mount, she was coming down the stairway. He then stood amazed at how beautiful she looked. Once she came downstairs, her mother introduced herself, "Hello, Ricky. Tamarra has told me so much about you. It is nice to finally meet you. I hope y'all have a good time."

"I just know we will. Thanks for letting Tamarra go to the dance with me." He then grabbed Tamarra's hand and said unto her, "The car is waiting."

They headed toward the car, got inside, and road off to the dance. Once they arrived at the high school hall, one of Tamarra's favorite songs was playing. She asked Rick would he like to dance with her.

He said, "I would but I do not know how to dance."

She said, "Do not worry about it. I will teach you how. It's really easy, just follow my lead."

At that moment, Rick felt as though he had found his best friend. When Tamarra looked into his eyes, she saw something else—she saw the love of her life. From that moment, they became the best of friends; they hung out together just about every day ever since their first school dance.

The next Sunday, Tamarra went to church with Rick at the Mount Zion Baptist Church where Momma Mamie and Uncle Pittman had served as preacher and first lady respectively for over thirty years. That morning too, Tamarra was surprised Rick led a song, singing with the church choir. She did not know that he sung as well as he did.

Once Rick reached the age of seventeen, Uncle Pittman decided that he needed his license. Uncle Pittman would take him and Tamarra out into the country to teach him how to drive; they had a great time in doing so. Once Rick received his license, Uncle Pittman took him down to the car dealership and bought him his first brand-new two-seater candy apple red Mercedes Benz. That day was the happiest day of his life! As soon as he got home, he rushed over to Tamarra's house to ask her father if she could take a ride with him in his new car. Once he got her father's approval, they road off into the sunset.

When Rick got into the eleventh grade, his Uncle Pittman's health began to fail him. Later, he had a very bad stroke that caused him to be hospitalized for several weeks.

Momma Mamie would have her Lady Club's meeting at the house every month on Wednesday at two o'clock sharp in the afternoon, with the Black elite ladies of New Orleans. The next day, while Uncle Pittman was out on the deck reading the Holy Word of God, Joe found him dead with his Bible in his hand. Momma Mamie sent Joe to pick up Rick from school. Once he heard the news about his uncle, it caused him to break down in tears. When Rick got home, Momma Mamie was sitting in the living quarters with her best friend Irene, crying. Rick rushed through the door of the living quarters, where she was sitting, with tears flowing from her eyes. Rick walked over and gave her a hug.

Momma Mamie said, "Baby honey child, Earl has just broken my heart. He just broke my little heart into pieces. Child, I just don't not know what I'm going to do, baby, now that the love of my life is gone to heaven far from me."

While Mommaa Mamie was preparing for the funeral, all of Uncle Pittman's relatives started coming in. Two of his sisters stayed at the house with Ricky and her. The two of them didn't really like Momma Mamie because they thought she was just marrying him for his money. But despite how they felt about her, she loved them the same as Uncle Pittman loved them. She had more class and was more beautiful than they were. Momma Mamie then called one of Uncle Pittman's old preacher friends to do the eulogy. She was so sad, but she managed to hold strong. That Sunday afternoon, the church was packed with preachers from all around. One of Uncle Pittman's preacher friends preached the Sunday morning service. The Mount Zion choir sang all of his favorite songs. Momma Mamie did not come to church that morning; she stayed home with Uncle Pittman's sisters, Mrs. Odessa and Mrs. Thelma. After morning service, the church had dinner at the church before the funeral. Ricky and Tamarra left the church to go back over to the house where Momma Mamie and her sisters-in-law were get ready for the funeral. Once all the cars got to the house for the funeral lineup, Joe got Momma Mamie's Bentley and brought it down to the front of the house and parked it in the front of the line behind the hearse. Then the funeral home director pulled him off stake, and they brought him out of the house and put him inside of the hearse. Momma Mamie held Pussy Wussy as Uncle Pittman's old preacher friend walked her out of the house along with his sisters, Rick, Tamarra, and family and friends following the coffin closely behind. There were a lot of people standing outside the house that day, watching as they put him inside the hearse. When they arrived at the church for the funeral services, the whole family walked inside the church. A friend of Reverend Pittman escorted Momma Mamie inside the church. She was nicely dressed. She had on a beautiful black and white hat and a black dress with matching gloves and shoes. Tears were flowing down her face. As she walked inside the church, all the people who were there stood and watched her. Once everyone was seated, the preacher called for Rick to come and sing a solo. Everyone was amazed at how well he sung. When the funeral was over, all of Momma Mamie's and Reverend Pittman's friends came over to the mansion for dinner. After everyone left that afternoon, Momma Mamie asked Uncle Pittman's sisters if they would stay a couple of days until the reading of the will.

A couple of days later, the lawyer came to Momma Mamie's house to discuss the will. When the lawyer began to read the will, he made known to them that Uncle Pittman's request was to leave each of his two sisters Seven hundred thousand dollars. To his nephew, Rick, a total of twenty million dollars with 50 percent shares of the A&B Oil Company. One of the stipulations on Rick's inheritance was that he would receive 20 percent of the monetary gifts, and the rest of the money, he will receive after he finishes college. Momma Mamie was left with 30 million in assistance and 50 percent shares in A&B Oil Company, along with 150 million dollars in monetary gifts. Also in Uncle Pittman's will, he wrote a special letter to Momma Mamie about the seed of the madam that stems from Momma Bea. The letter goes as follows:

> To my darling Madam that has superseded the legacy of Momma Bea by it being that you are the quaintness of a lady, there has not been a successor chosen to fill the obligations given to me by God as the preacher of the Mount Zion Baptist Church. I leave you the keys to the kingdom of God to choose with the assistance of the deacon board in finding such a man who is sound in doctrine that will preach the pure Gospel of Jesus Christ.

Before they left the conference room, Uncle Pittman's old preacher friend walked up to Mamie and said unto her, "Since I'm in retirement, I think that I would be the best man to look after you and the Mount Zion Baptist Church."

Momma Mamie then said unto him in a state of mourning, "My darling Earl has not even been in the ground for a week, and here it is that you come looking after his wife and his church. You peasant of a man, I dare you." She then turned and walked off.

The next day after the reading of the will, Uncle Pittman's sisters headed back to Alabama, telling Momma Mamie as they entered into the car, "Call us now, child, so we can keep in touch."

In the back of Momma Mamie's mind, she knew they were two-faced and didn't really like her, so she put on her good face and said, "Okay, ladies," and they then drove off in the car.

Chapter 7

Later on that morning, after her sisters-in-law left, she decided to have a cup of coffee out on the back deck to reminisce about her husband, as she looked out over her beautiful flower garden. When Rick came downstairs before school, he found her sitting out on the deck in deep meditation. When she noticed that he was in her presence, she said unto him, "Hi, son, are you about ready for school?"

"Yes."

"Have a seat." There was a smile across her face, as if he was her last hope of happiness. "Now that you are approaching your twelfth grade, have you thought about what it is that you want to do after you graduated?"

"No, not really."

"Well, son, you need to start thinking about what you want to do after you graduate. The time is drawing near child. It is about time you realize that you have a company to run. Maybe you should think about going to college and studying business management.

"I'll think about it."

"In the meantime, I will be looking for you a nice university to attend. I want you to use that money that your uncle gave you wisely. The reason he left you those gifts from God was because he believed in you to do the right thing with your life and for you to be the best you can be for God and your career. We both want you to go to college and do your best in getting your education. Baby honey child, when I'm gone, all this will be yours, all that we've worked for all of our lives. Tell me something, how is Tamarra, honey? That is one fine young lady. I can tell she likes you a lot. Don't you let that girl pass you by."

"We are just friends. Now I must rush off to school."

On his way to his car, he kissed her and then rushed off. Then she got up to get dressed and prepare herself for the meeting with the board members that would take place at twelve o'clock that afternoon at her house. When the members began to arrive at her house, they all were seated in the conference room until Momma Mamie came in. Once Momma Mamie entered the doors of the conference room, she was carrying a manila envelope in her hand. Everyone stood, bowing their heads as if she had the veil of God around about her head. When she took her seat, everyone else sat. When it came to handling business, Momma Mamie was the lady for the job. Although she was not a self-seeking individual, she believed in doing what it took to please God. She was as humble as a lamb; she never placed judgment on anyone. Anything that Momma Mamie did when it came to dealing with people, she would tell you what was right. Then she would leave it in your hands to make the right decision. Because of this mentality, she was loved and respected by all who knew her. When she took her seat, she said unto the men in the room,

"Good morning, fellow saints of God. The God of heaven and earth has taken our preacher and my darling Earl like Joshua superseded Moses. Oh, dear children of the cloth, we need to choose a man of God to supersede our preacher Revered Earl Pittman. We all know that Earl has worked very hard to build this church up from nothing. It brings me great joy to know that you all have served him well. In choosing the next preacher for the Mount Zion Baptist Church, we cannot be self-seeking in doing so. I'll have you to know that in the process of choosing him, the door for the position will be open for all of those persons who desire the position. The man chosen for the position will not have to want for anything as long as he preaches sound doctrine and he is faithful until the end. You all know that even I am in old age. Once I am gone, the deeds of the church will be left into the hands of my nephew, Rick Smith. Once she made this statement, everyone in the room went to whispering in each other's ears.

The eldest deacon, Carl Johnson, said unto Momma Mamie, "Oh humble lady of God, whom God has allowed to be overseer of his kingdom until the man of God has been chosen, It would be lawful that the madam who has superseded the legacy of Momma Bea leaves the church deeds in the hands of the saints that have been with it since its beginning?"

Momma Mamie then responded, "Oh servant of God, may God be glorified. When a king dies, will he not leave the things in which he has worked for and built into the hands of one who is not connected with his bloodline, or will he leave his life works in the hands of another man's bloodline that is not connected with his own."

The deacon responded, "He will leave it to the bloodline attached with his own."

Momma Mamie then said unto them, "Now, you dear men, understand why I have made the decision that I have made."

Everyone in the room said amen.

Another deacon asked, "Who will preach in the meantime until another preacher is found?"

Momma Mamie said, "I will leave that in the hands of Elder Fry. Whenever he deems it necessary for the assistant ministers to preach, by it being that we only have two assistant preachers at Mount Zion, we'll let him decide which one will fill in on Sunday until the next preacher is found."

Everyone agreed with the decision that Momma Mamie made.

As time progressed, Rick's graduation day was fast approaching. Rick was so excited he was finally about to graduate from high school. When he got home that afternoon, he ate dinner with Momma Mamie and Tamarra. They discussed what they were going to do after high school. Tamarra made known that her plans were to go to Oberlin College in Oberlin, Ohio, to study nursing. Rick later found out that he would be attending Cheyney University to get his degree in business management. On the night of the graduation in the summer of 1942, after Rick walked across the stage, he went outside to find a GLE Class Coupe that Momma Mamie had purchased for him for his graduation present. That night, Rick did not know that Momma Mamie had invited the whole senior class and their parents over to their house on the back lawn for a graduation party.

In the fall of the year in, he began packing too, getting ready to go to Cheyney, Pennsylvania to attend school. That afternoon, Momma Mamie came into his room and said to him, "Son, ever since you came into this house, you have filled my heart with happiness and joy. You have not caused me one ounce of grief, for this I'm proud of you. I have a favor to ask of you. Don't go out there into this world of sin and break my heart because this old heart of mine cannot take any more, baby. My soul would just leave my old wrinkle body. Baby honey child, it would just leave my body, so, son, go out there and give life your best and do not let the love in your heart deceive you of heaven. Because in the end, heaven is all you got to look forward to. One thing else, son, do not forget to bring your old Momma Mamie a madam that will supersede the legacy of Momma Bea." She then kissed him on his forehead and went about doing her duties around the house.

Later on during the week, he and Tamarra played tennis. That same night, they went to the lookout point and sat in his two-seater Mercedes with the top down, looking out across the sky, to say their last good-byes before they went away to college. Rick liked Tamarra a lot, but she loved him more. She felt as if she had fallen in love with him that night while they were sitting in the car, looking out into the sky at the stars and the moon.

She said to him, "Rick I think I have fallen in love with you. You are the type of man a woman dreams of being with."

He then began to express his feelings to her. When he began to talk, she noticed in his eyes that his feelings were not equivalent to hers. She then put her finger over his mouth and said, "There is no need at this moment to express to me how it is that you feel about me." She then kissed him gently and laid their seats back and continued kissing each other.

The day after, Rick began putting his luggage in the trunk of his car. Momma Mamie told him that she would send the rest of his things later. Once he was packed and ready to go, Momma Mamie was standing on the front porch. She then told him before he left, "Now, son, go out there and be a man and make your momma proud."

When he got ready to drive off, Joe and Earlene the maid were standing out on the front porch with Momma Mamie, waving good-bye to him as he left. Momma Mamie's eyes were filled with tears of joy.

Chapter 8

Rick's first two weeks in college were great. He met a new group of friends; one of them was even a captain of football team. Later on, he joined their fraternity. Momma Mamie called him to let him know that in a couple of days, she would be traveling down to visit him. When Momma Mamie arrived to his college, she and Joe were both excited to see him. They took a walk around the campus by it being the college she went to thirty years ago. She was really excited to see the new changes the college had made. Joe sat down on a bench while Rick and her walked and spent time together, talking.

Momma Mamie and Rick took a seat on the bench under the shade trees, as she looked across the beautiful landscape of the campus. She said unto him, "Child, I have always dreamed of having a child that could come from my own womb, that would grow up and come to such a fine university like this. The good Lord above has allowed you to come along and take that child's place of my barren womb. If Momma Bea could see you now, her heart would just be bubbling over with joy. I am reminded of a young man, by the name of Langston Hughes, who once said, "I am the darker brother. They send me to the kitchen to eat. When company comes, but I laugh and eat well and grow strong. Tomorrow, I'll be able to sit down at the table when company comes. Nobody'll dare tell me, 'Eat in the kitchen.' They'll see how beautiful I am and be ashamed—I, too, am America." Baby, these words in which I have spoken from the echo of this fine young man, gives us hope as black people to be our best in whatever dreams we have set for ourselves. When it comes to being someone in this fine land in which we live called America. Baby, once you have climbed the academic ladder of achievement, all men will respect you as an individual, whether you are black or white."

Rick then asked Momma Mamie, "What did you mean when you asked me if I could give you a madam that supersedes the legacy of Momma Bea?"

Momma Mamie begins telling him the history that lied behind the veil of the madam. "Momma Bea was a daughter of a slave. You're great-grandma, Momma Bulla, her momma was a very beautiful woman. She fell madly in love with the slave master, Master Armstrong. He too was madly in love with her. To this union, a child was born, named Momma Bea. When the slave master's wife found out that Momma Bulla was pregnant, Momma Bulla worked as a house Negro, the slave master's wife ordered Poppa Armstrong to remove Momma Bulla out of the house, putting her into the fields with the field Negroes. Once Momma Bea was born and reached the age of five, the slave master's wife sunk out of the house in the middle of the night into the hut where Momma Bulla was sleeping and cut her throat from ear to ear with the intent to kill

Momma Bea as well. Master Armstrong stopped her in the nick of time and brought Momma Bea inside his home and raised her as if she was a white child. Momma Bea was a very light-skinned woman who could have passed for a white woman. It was not easy for her to live inside the house with her stepmother and older sister for they made it very hard for her. She loved Bertha, her baby sister, and Jim, her little brother, very much, and they loved her as well. Shortly after Momma Bulla's murder, Momma Bea did not have to work as a slave because Poppa Armstrong made it clear to the family that she was an equal, and no one would ever mistreat her. Unfortunately, no one in the city knew that she was a daughter of a slave for Madam Armstrong knew if any one found out that her husband had a baby by a slave and that they were raising her as their daughter, it would have brought shame on their family. When Poppa Armstrong died, he left Momma Bea a large amount of money and the plantation in his will. When the reading of the will was done, Madam Armstrong kept it hidden from her and dared her children not to tell her about the will. Mrs. Armstrong later gave Momma Bea two hundred dollars and sent her away on a train to Montgomery, Alabama, to live. Once she got there, she worked as a maid for a dancer. From work, she saved enough money up to put herself through nursing school. At that time in history, it was unheard of any black women going to school. Because of Momma Bea's skin tone it was quiet easy for her to pass for a white woman, and she did not tell them any different. She knew inside her soul that she was a black woman, and she was proud of it. When she graduated, she met and married a young white attorney by the name of Curtis Flowers. During their marriage, she kept from him the fact that she was a black woman. They later had two daughters, Momma Georgia and Momma Chaney, who died at childbirth. When Mamie and Ernestine were little girls playing on the front porch, Momma Bea was about one hundred and three years old. A white man came by Momma Bea's house and asked us where is our mother? We told him that she was inside the house. He then walked up on the porch and knocked on the door.

When Momma came to the door, he asked Momma Georgia, "I am look for Madam Bea. Is she here?"

She then asked him who wants to know.

He then said, "Her sister has driven a long distance to see her to discuss an important matter with her."

Momma Georgia said, "Her sister? Momma Bea didn't have a sister!"

At that time, Momma Bea was sitting out on the back porch in her rocking chair, nodding in the evening sun. Momma Georgia said unto the white man, "Wait one minute while I go and fetch her."

Momma Georgia went out on the back porch where Momma Bea was sitting and awakened her. "Momma, you have a visitor that wants to see you about an important matter."

Momma Bea said, "Who is it, child?"

"This white man says that it is your sister."

Momma Bea rose up out of her chair as if old age had no hold on her. "Tell me, child, where is she?"

"She's outside sitting inside the car, waiting to see you."

"Which one could it every be? Did he say a name, child?" Tears rolled from the pits of Momma Bea's eyes.

"No, Momma, he did not give a name."

With excitement in her veins, she said unto Momma Georgia, "Tell her to come inside so I can look up on her beautiful face once more!"

Momma Georgia walked Momma Bea to her room, and she went back to the front door and told the white man to bring her inside. He then went back to the car to help the old woman out of her expensive white car. When she got out of the car, once Ernestine and me saw her, we stopped playing, caught in amazement. When she got out of the car, she looked as if she was Momma Bea's twin, the only difference was, she was a white woman. Her hair was as white as snow. Her eyes were as dim as the morning sun—it was as if the burden of time had hit her right down the center of her back. As she approached the steps of the porch, Momma Bea approached the screen door and stopped briefly to look to see which sister it was. When she walked outside on her porch that afternoon, it was as if her youthfulness had been restored. She went inside her room and pushed her hair up in a knot and then put on her best Sunday hat and white gloves. When they looked in each other's eyes, the wells of their eyes were full with tears.

Momma Bea said, "Bertha, hon, is that you, child?"

Bertha said, "Hon, yes, child, it's me!"

When Momma Bertha walked up on the porch where Momma Bea was standing, they hugged each other for a long time with tears falling from their eyes. Momma Bertha said unto her, "Baby honey child, my guilt has caused me to keep myself hidden from you for many years, and my heart child has been broken into pieces ever since the last time I seen your pretty smile."

Momma Bea said unto her, "Hon, need not to weary for the devil has been busy for many years. All that matters now is that you're here."

They then grabbed each other's hand, and Momma Bea said unto her, "Let's go on the back porch and have some tea, child." Momma Georgia had the maid to prepare tea for them. "It's been a long time child since I last saw you."

Madam Bertha said, "I know, child. My heart has been broken ever since Momma sent you away from my heart and Jim's. It just broke my soul into pieces, child. I didn't know where you had gone."

"How is Jim?

"Hon, Jim died ten years ago from a massive heart attack."

Momma Bea became very silent. "Child, it's good to see that you are still a beautiful lady."

"Child, it isn't easy being a lady. My Bea...aren't your little madams gorgeous?"

Then Ernestine and I began to smile. Momma Bea introduced us to our great aunt. She told her our names.

Momma Bertha then said unto us, "Come and sit on Momma Bertha's lap so I can have a better look at y'all."

When I sat on her lap, she looked into my eyes and said to Momma Bea, "Child, she has Poppa's eye." And tears rolled down her face. Momma Bea called for Momma Georgia and Poppa Sam, me, and Ernestine's father—he was a black man—so they could meet aunt Bertha.

Momma Bertha said unto Momma Georgia, "Child you have brought us some fine young ladies into this world. Hon, you look just like your grand Momma Bulla." She then turned and looked at Momma Bea and said, "Bea, it's good to know, child, that the black madam is still continuing to live on after legacy of yo' Momma Bulla."

She then let us down out her lap and Momma Bea then said unto us, "Go, my darling angels, and play a while and do not get your white dress and gloves dirty." Momma Georgia took us back into the front of the house, leaving them alone to talk.

Momma Bertha said, "Bea, how have you been, child? It looks like you have done well for yourself."

Momma Bea said, "Child, it was my husband, Curtis, was a very good provider for me and Georgia. God rest his soul. And you? Did you ever get married, Bertha?"

Bertha said, "Why yes, child! I had been married for over seventy-two years, child, to a man by the name of Sir Isaac Taylor. We had a beauty life together and two beautiful daughters, Elaine and Mary."

"I bet they are just angels."

Momma Bertha reached inside her purse. "I have some pictures with me. Do you want to see them, hon?"

Momma Bea looked at the pictures and began to cry. "They are lovely."

"One day, hon. I will bring them to see you."

"Hon, do they know?"

"When they were little girls, child, I would sing them the song you, me, and little Jim sang when we ran and played out in the sapins of Poppa's field. I would tell them often the story of my long lost niggar sister. It is their desire to see you now that I have found you."

"How is Momma and Madam Mary?"

"God rest their souls. Momma died about fifteen years ago on her deathbed. She called out for you, child, saying unto us, 'Baby honey child, where is that niggar child of mine?' She was looking into my eyes for she knew how much I loved you. 'If ya'll ever see her, tell her that I asked God to forgive my soul. I want you to ask her to forgive me for the great sins I have done to her and her mother, out of my rage for love. May the good Lord above bless her children.' Baby, you know, Jim never forgave Momma and Mary for what they done to you. From hearing those words that Momma spoke in that room that day, tears filled his eyes, and he walked out of the room before she closed her eyes to greet that great good-bye in the sky. Mary shortly died a couple of years later of a high fever."

Momma Bea wept in her heart. She loved them regardless of how they treated her; they were all she knew as her family.

Momma Bertha reached inside her purse, "Hon, I have something to give you. I have come to give you something that is rightfully yours, child. For many years, the devil had taken over my soul being, influenced by Momma. We have kept this from you for many years, child. When daddy died, he left you some money and the deeds to the plantation."

Momma Bea said with tears in her eyes, "Child, my heart told me that Poppa gave me something because he loved me just like he loved y'all. When Momma Armstrong told me to leave ya'll, honey baby child, it just broke my heart into pieces."

"Baby, I just couldn't go on with this secret to my grave, for I knew the good Lord above was watching down on my soul. So I had to find you, child, if it killed me to do so. I have traveled very far to give Poppa's gifts to you."

Bertha then reached inside her purse and pulled out an envelope and handed it to Momma Bea. At that moment, Momma Bea's eyes were filled with tears.

James Brumley

Momma Bertha then decided to stay with us for a week. She and Momma Bea went to New Orleans along with me, Ernestine, and Momma Georgia to see their house that they were raised up in as little girls. When they arrived at the house, it looked like no one had lived in it for many years. When we drove up to the front of the abandoned house, Momma Bertha said unto Momma Bea, "Bea, child, here is you and your daughter home. Poppa would have wanted to be this same."

Momma Bea said unto her, "Baby honey child, this is the home not only for my child but for you darlings as well. That the way Poppa would have had it. You and your daughter have just as much right here as me and my girls do."

Bertha cried. "It shall be done, hon."

When Momma Bea and Momma Bertha entered the house, the flames of their memories began to rise. Momma Bea began to cry because of the overwhelming memories of living there as a little girl. Momma Bertha had tears in her eyes as she looked at an old picture of her mother, sister, brother, and father. There was also a very old picture of Momma Bula and Poppa Armstrong in a dusty and worn-out photo album hidden away in one of Poppa Armstrong's old chest boxes. Momma Bea didn't want to live inside the house; she just paid the taxes on it until she died.

Momma Bea told us the day when she died, "I want you two girls to grow up and move back home to this house so that the legacy of the black madam can live on through the seed of Momma Bulla. Could you girls give me a madam that will supersede the legacy of Momma Bea?"

The reason she asked us that question was that when she was a little girl, she would see Momma Bulla prancing around the slave house with a white dress that Poppa Armstrong had brought her. She would pretend to be a lady, like that of white women. She also knew that she could never become his wife, so she would dance around the hut and pretend in her convinced heart that she was the lady and wife of Poppa Armstrong. She would ask Momma Bea that when was a little girl, "Will you give me a madam that will supersede the legacy of you, Momma."

This saying stemmed from Momma Bulla's lust for Poppa Armstrong. After Momma Bulla's vicious murder, the black madam became cursed. It happened because of their lust for one another and the great sin that Poppa Armstrong's great-grandfather had done to a slave woman who had a child for him a long time ago.

Rick said unto his Momma Mamie, "Momma, tell me about the slave and the sin?"

Momma Mamie said unto him, "Now is not the time, child. You will find out in due time all about the slave's sin. For now, all you need to do is live a pure life, son, and you will be just fine. Baby, the Lord has looked up on me and protected my heart from that curse. If you live a good life, there is one thing that you need to worry about. I there is one thing I have learned to know in this world—my day shall surely come. I am the last madam living. Since Lorene passed away, the seed of the madam is left in your hands, to give the world the madam that will supersede the legacy of Momma Bea. The white madam still lives on, child. I don't know where, but she lives through the seed of Poppa Jim, Momma Bertha, and Momma Mary. It is left up to you now to make sure the black madam lives on through seed of Momma Bea."

After she finished telling him the history of the black madam, she became tired. Rick drove her and Joe back to the hotel where they were staying.

Later on that night, Rick and Gerard went to a party with the football team. After hanging out, they went back to Rick's apartment. Both of them were already pretty drunk from the party, yet they began to drink some more while watching boxing on the television. In Gerard's excitement in watching the boxing match on television, he grabbed Rick's knees. Rick couldn't say anything, as if his tongue locked from the shock that ran up his legs from Gerard's touch. Gerard then looked at Rick because of his mixed feelings of his god-given manhood of duties; he forfeited it due to the lust that filled his heart and kissed Rick on his neck and across the lips. Rick didn't try to fight him off because it felt good to him; he never had this feeling before, he liked it. From that point, one thing led to another. He and Rick had sex even though they really didn't know what they were doing at first, but it felt good to them both. They started to hang out even more and liked each other. They later moved in with each other. One night, Rick came home from hanging out with some friends. Once he got home, he noticed that all the light was out inside his apartment, and Gerald's car was parked inside the driveway. Once he unlocked the door and walked inside, he turned on the living room light and noticed that Gerald was not there. He then figured that he was just asleep inside their bedroom. He then walked to the bedroom and opened the door. He found Gerard in bed—with a woman. Rick began to scream at the top of his voice, saying, "Who is this bitch in my bed?"

Gerard could not say anything because he was busted. The woman he was sleeping with said, "Who is this guy?"

Gerald began to explain when Rick interrupted him, "He is my boyfriend."

The woman then said, "What?"

Rick picked up a lamp and a clock and threw it at them both. At that moment, the woman managed to escape with her clothes in her hand. She said unto Gerard, "What is this? You like men?"

Gerard stood speechless.

Rick then said unto him, "How could you do this to me? I have giving you my love and you do this to me. Get out of my house right now and don't you ever come back! And I want you to leave my keys to the car and the house on the table before you leave. GET OUT NOW!"

Gerard grabbed his things and left, walking. Rick then fell down on his knees and began to cry. They broke up for a while, but Rick could not stop thinking about him. They got back together, but things only got worse between them. Gerard would drink and fight Rick all the time until Rick could not take it anymore. When Rick decided to leave Gerard, it broke his heart into pieces. Rick raised his grades to straight As. Because Rick loved Momma Mamie, he stayed on the honor roll and finally graduated from college with a bachelor's degree in business and management.

When it came for Rick's graduation, he was twenty-two years old at the time. When Momma Mamie arrived, she was excited to see Rick doing something positive with his life. Because of his positive efforts, she bought him a new ring for his graduation present. With tears in her eyes she said, "I am so proud of you. The Lord in heaven is smiling down on you, child."

Chapter 9

After Rick's graduation, he decided to move to Miami, Florida, where he later met and fell in love with a young man by the name of Steven, who ended up becoming worse than Gerard, his ex-boyfriend. Steven was also a heavy drinker; he would have big parties where they would sniff cocaine, even causing Rick to become addicted as well. Life became very difficult for Rick in dealing with this young man. One night, during one of their parties, the police raided the apartment, looking for drugs. Once the police busted through the doors, everyone began to run. Rick ran and hid in the closet, between his clothes. The police searched the house over and didn't find him. They took everyone else inside the apartment to jail, including Steven. Rick knew that it was just a matter time before the police came; he just didn't know when. Once Rick realized that there wasn't anyone in the house, he decided to come out of the closet from where he was, hiding scared and frightened with tears running out his eyes. He knew deep down inside he was living the wrong type of life. At this point, he felt as if he reached his end. He needed help.

He didn't want to call his aunt Mamie, because he had not talked to her in a long time. He needed to talk to someone about the things that were troubling his soul. He did not know what was wrong with him that caused him to be in the situation that he was in. He said in the middle of his fear unto himself, *Why me Lord? All I was trying to do was just to love.* He then grabbed the phone and fell down on his knees pressed against the wall and began dialing his aunt Mamie's number for help, for he knew that she had the answer that would solve the dark mysteries of his mind. It was two weeks before Christmas when he called her.

Momma Mamie answered the phone; to her surprise, it was Rick on the other line. "Hi, baby! I have not heard from you in quite awhile. Is everything well with you, son? I have been very worried about you. I was thinking, child, that the curse has gotten you."

"No, Momma Mamie, no curse is ever going to get me. Everything is fine," Rick replied, knowing in his heart that he had tremendous problems.

"Are you coming home for Christmas?"

Rick had been using drugs for weeks at a time; he had forgotten what time of year it was. "Oh yes, Momma Mamie, I'll be coming home for Christmas."

"That's great, child! I will have the caterer prepare dinner for us. Do you have any friends that you want to bring, child?"

"No, Momma, just me."

When Rick arrived in New Orleans at Momma Mamie's house, he rang the doorbell, and Joe answered the door. When he looked at Rick, it was as if he had seen a ghost by it being that Rick had lost so much weight. Rick then walked inside house to the study and found Momma

Mamie reading her Bible. Once she recognized that he had entered inside her study, she laid down her Bible and looked up at him, pulling of her reading glasses. "Baby honey child, what has happened to you? You look like you have not rested or eaten in days. Child, come here to me." She held him in her arms. "Baby, have you been letting this old wicked world messing with your heart?"

All Rick could do is cry on her shoulders. "Yes, Momma, yes."

"It's okay, baby. Momma Mamie is here now."

Momma Mamie never asked him about what he was going through; it was as if she already knew. Rick, after crying on her shoulder, decided to go upstairs and go to bed. The next day, he slept until about noon. When he awoke, Momma Mamie had Lady prepare a large breakfast for him. When he came downstairs, he smelled the food. He went into the dining quarters where Momma Mamie was waiting on him. Once his plate was fixed, he began eating as if hadn't eaten in weeks. He pushed the food down his throat like a wild savage. All Momma Mamie could do was look and shake her head, knowing in the back of her mind that the curse sent down from Momma Bea was trying to take the breath of life out of him. That morning before Rick awoke, she called a psychiatrist, hoping that he could help Rick with his problems. After Rick finished eating, Momma Mamie told him, "Once the holidays are over, I have gotten you an appointment to meet and talk to a doctor about what it is your going through."

Rick then said to Momma Mamie, "I'll be fine. I don't need to talk to a doctor about what I am going through. I can do it by myself."

"You are going to see that doctor because I'm not going too lose you to the grips of the curse. I have lost Ernestine and Lorene, and I will not lose you. Do you hear me? I do not want to hear nothing else about you not wanting to see this doctor. Do you hear me, child? And that is final."

Rick then paused and said, "Yes, Momma."

When Christmas came around, Momma Mamie had a Christmas party on Christmas Eve for all of her friends—black and white—everyone was there. The next day when Rick awoke and came downstairs, he didn't find Momma Mamie inside the house. He then went outside on the back deck and found Momma Mamie reading her Bible. She then looked up at him and said, "How are you doing, son?"

"I am doing great!"

"I have something to give you." She then called for Mrs. Butler and asked him to bring Rick his Christmas present.

Rick said unto to her, "You did not have to do that, Momma."

"It was nothing."

When Joe brought the gift out to him, Rick was excited to see what was inside. When he opened it, there was a black Bible inside.

"Thank you, Momma. I needed this because I do not have one of my own at home."

"I know, son. You know you have a meeting with that doctor today."

Rick said, "Yes, Momma, I know."

"Son, you know that your Momma Mamie is not crazy. My old eyes have seen many things, and the good Lord above has given me wisdom. A fine man like yourself, all these pretty girls out here to choose from, why haven you picked you one? How is that girl Tamarra doing? Have you talked to her lately?"

Rick couldn't say anything. "No, I had lost contact with her over the years."

"Tell me something, son, do you desire the body of man?

Rick's heart began to beat fast with a loss for words. All he could think to himself was, *How is it that she knows?* He then said, "Momma, I do." He could not lie too her.

"Son, you know I am very happy this morning because the Lord told me last night through my conscience that everything would be well with you. I am blessed this morning because you have come to me with your burdens, enabling me to help you. Sometimes I say to myself, if only Ernestine and Lorene would have come to me with the things that troubled their souls maybe the good Lord above would have allowed me to help them before the curse of the madam consumed them in death. Baby, the things that makes my soul tremble is that you lust after a body of a man. You know that this is a great sin before God, but your life is between you and God. The question that lies in the back of my mind is, how will the seed of the black madam live on through you if you desire to go against the nature of all that God has attend for a man to be."

Rick then said unto her, "Someway, somehow, I'd give you a madam that would supersede the legacy of Momma Bea.

"In time. I hope so, son."

At that moment, Momma Mamie put the fate of the black madam in Rick's hands. She then said again, "Okay, child. After you get through with your session with the doctor, you need to start thinking about your responsibility with the company that your Uncle Pittman left us. Before you go back home to Miami, I want to take you down to the company and show you around so you can meet your employees."

"Okay, Momma. I want you to know that everything is going to be all right."

"I hope, child, I hope. Go on now and get yourself ready to meet that doctor."

Chapter 10

As Rick got up to go back inside the house, Momma Mamie said, "You know, child, the desire of your heart is not right in the eyesight of God."

Rick then said, "I know, Momma, I know."

"I want you to know one thing. I'm not going to beat you over the head, about your lifestyle. I'm going to leave that business with you and God, child."

Being consumed by the lust of his heart, the words Mamie spoke unto him that day went into one ear and out the other. A couple of weeks later, Rick got well from his drug addiction and his mental restraints with the help of the doctor. Momma Mamie called for a board meeting with the company so they could meet their new boss Rick Smith. Rick didn't have to work hard or be at the office at all because Jiffery the CEO took care of the company for him. Any major decisions made for the company, he would have to talk to Momma Mamie and Rick about them. A couple of days later, Rick decided it was time that he goes back to Miami. Before he left, Momma Mamie said to him,

"Now, son, don't go out there and let the world play with your heart again."

When he got back to Miami, he was drug-free and looking ever better than before. He did not contact Steven anymore and later found out that he had went to prison. He also ran into a drag queen by the name of Diamond who worked as a dancer for a nightclub. When Diamond saw Rick, he was standing in a corner all by himself. The first thing Diamond said unto him was, "Girl, you are beautiful."

Rick then said, "Excuse me?"

"Pay me no mind, baby. I'm just crazy. What's your name, honey?"

"Rick."

"They call me Diamond around here. Say let's have a drink."

They had a drink together, and soon after that, they became the best of friends. Diamond will tell him all the time that he was beautiful and that he would make a beautiful lady. Because it was a world that Rick was not familiar with, he would never dress up in women's clothing. But there was something inside him, telling him that he wanted to do so. So finally, Diamond convinced him to let her give him a total makeover. He decided to let Diamond create the new madam who would supersede the legacy of Momma Bea. At that moment, Rick hadn't realized what it was that he was doing, but he was transforming himself into the next madam who would supersede the dream of his family. He and Diamond went out to shop for new clothes, to give him his first makeover; he was so excited. Rick already had a long pretty hair; he didn't need to put on a wig. Once Diamond finished his makeover, she then handed him a mirror. When he looked at himself, he noticed he was a beautiful woman.

Diamond was amazed by his beauty. "Child, get out of here. If I was straight, I would try to get at you, honey. I told you that you would make a pretty lady with the touch of my hand of beauty. Girl, you are going to let them boys have it."

From that point on, Rick would go to the nightclubs to see Diamond perform. The year was 1947. Rick became interested in performing in the nightclubs like Diamond, by it being that he had a beautiful voice and the looks—he would do an excellent job in doing so. Diamond thought that when he told her about his desire to dance and sing, it was a great idea. Diamond set him up with the club owner so they can set a date for him to perform. The club owner knew of Rick's secret; however, he agreed to let him do so because he had his own personal agenda in mind for him. When the boss told him yes, he was so excited that he would be performing for the first time.

Diamond then played some music and said unto him, "Show me what you got." After hearing him sing and perform in the living room of his apartment, she was amazed with his talent. "Girl, it has been in your shy face all the time." They then smiled at each other.

The night before Ricky's big day, Diamond took him to the beauty shop of one of his home girls to get a new hairdo and a new makeover for his performance. That night on their way to the club, Diamond said, "Girl, you do not have a stage name. We have to come up with a name for you. What will we call you?"

Rick said, "Call me Madam Colleen."

When Rick performed that night, all the men in the club loved him, not knowing that he too was really not a woman, but a man. He didn't have to use any extra vocals to his song; he sang with his natural voice. When he and Diamond got to the club that night while Diamond was doing the finishing touching on him before his performance, she was amazed once again. "You know, baby, your stage name fit your beautiful face."

He then looked at the handsomeness and the femininity of his mother, shining on his face, and smiled. From that point on, he performed more times, and the men loved him to the point that they thought of him as a goddess. Rick loved dressing up like that of a woman, so much so that he began to dress like a woman every day.

During that time, he started dating the club owner Raymond, who started to like him also. They dated for a while, and he then later moved in with Raymond who also used drugs and caused him to use drugs again. One night when Rick got in from the club, he and Raymond got into an argument. Raymond slapped him across the face, knocking him into the wall. From that point, things got worse between them both. Raymond continued to beat him; he beat Rick one time so bad that he broke Rick's jaw, blackened his eyes, and broke his arm, causing him to be put in the hospital for several weeks. While Rick was in the hospital, Diamond came to visit him. At that moment, Rick knew that he needed to make some changes in his life, or he'll end up dead. During Diamond's visit with him, she asked him, "How are you doing, girl?"

Rick said, "Girl, a little beat up that's all."

Raymond had gotten so jealous he had stop Rick from talking with Diamond.

Diamond said, "Girl...I told you the first time when that niggar jumped on you, you should have left him alone then!"

"I know, girl, but I was in love with him."

"Girl, love isn't going to get you nowhere but dead! If I was you, I would get out this hospital and go back to that house and wait until that nigga goes to sleep and boil me some hot grits and pour them all over that nigga. And I bet you he would think twice before he hit you again, girl. Hmmm."

"Girl, you know I can't do that to him. I love him too much."

Rick did not call Momma Mamie because he did not want her to worry about him for he felt that he could handle his problems on his own. Diamond finally convinced him not to go back to Raymond, fearful that Raymond would kill him the next time. When Rick got out of the hospital, he moved his things out of Raymond's house without him knowing. He then moved with Diamond to get away from him.

About a year later, Rick decided he did not want to dress like a man anymore. He wanted to continue dressing as a lady permanently, so he told Diamond about his desire, and she told him to go for it. At the time, he did not know how to tell Momma Mamie about the changes in his life. He was hesitant in telling her for he knew that it would break her heart into pieces. Deep down, he knew that it was the wrong thing to do. In keeping this secret to himself, not telling Momma Mamie about it, Rick knew he had not seen her in a very long time because of how he was living his life, dressing in women clothing. He decided that he would keep himself away from her until he was to tell her. After a couple months passed, he had decided that it was the right time to tell her about his decision. He then decided to call her and tell her he wanted to come home to visit; Momma Mamie was very glad to hear from him. Within the next two weeks, he traveled back to New Orleans to see her, stripping himself of his woman attire, to look like his original self as a man.

Chapter 11

When he arrived in New Orleans at Momma Mamie's house, she was so happy to see him. During dinner that afternoon, he and Momma Mamie sat down and began to talk. She asked him, "Child, how have you been living?"

Rick said, "Everything is fine."

"Have you been viewing those reports that Jiffery has been sending you?"

"Yes, Jiff is doing a great job in taking care of the company."

"Yes, he has been doing a good job. I would like for you to move here and run that business yourself."

"Not now, Momma Mamie. I have a lot of business that I need too take care of back at home but one day maybe."

"It's good that you're still looking well, son."

"Thank you, Momma. Momma Mamie, I have something very important to talk to you about."

"What is it, child?"

Rick then pushed his chair from the table and walked over to get him some more fruit from the fruit table. As he put the fruit on his plate, he said, "I have been thinking about this for a long time."

"What, child?"

"I want you to know for the past seven years, I have been living my life dressing and dancing as a woman, and I want to live my life as a woman."

"Child, have you lost your everlasting mind, child!"

"I knew you would be upset with me…but I'm telling you these things because I don't want to keep it from you."

"Come sit down next to me, child. You know, child, how I feel about this great sin that has taken over your mind. It's just not right in the eyesight of God. I am not going to try and stop you because I know you are going to do what you want to do no matter what I say."

Momma Mamie did not want to push Rick away by trying to stop him from following his lustful desires for she knew if he could not confide in her, he would begin to confide in the world. She also wanted to keep his heart near to her so that she could try and protect his head from the curse of the madam that has haunted the family for many years. At that moment, as the words of wisdom ran through Momma Mamie's mind, she said, "We do need another madam in the family. What you would call yourself?"

Rick said, "Madam Colleen."

"Child, you are putting me in a very uncomfortable situation." As she looked up at the heavens, she said, "Lord, have mercy on my soul. If the people at the church found out, I believe I would just faint."

"They won't find out, Mother, because the next time when I come back to New Orleans, I will be fully dressed as Colleen, your long lost niece."

Momma Mamie shook her head, saddened from the words spoken by him. "Okay, child, I hope you know what it is that you are doing. It is my prayer, child, that you change your ways before the good Lord above take your life from you." She hugged him and continued, "May God be with you, child. When you come back down to visit, we'll go shop at some of my favorite department stores. If you are going to be a lady, baby honey child, you are the best lady ever. In the meantime, I will be praying for you and your soul."

Within the next few days, Rick went back to Miami. After he left, Momma Mamie had a talk with Joe. She sat down out on the back deck of the mansion. "Rick and I had a talk before he left that he wants to live his life dressing like that of a woman. That child has lost his mind to the devil, and he about too worry my mind pink. I did not try to stop him because I wanted to keep him near to me. I feel that I will be able to help him before it's too late. I just hope that God will give me the strength to do so before he calls my name."

Joe said unto her, "Madam, some time it is best to leave matters like this in the hand of your God and let him take care of it. He had never let you down in the pasted."

Chapter 12

Once Rick arrived at Diamond's apartment, he saw her sitting inside the living room. He laid his bags on the table. "Girl, I finally told my Momma Mamie about what I want."

"Girl, what did...she say?"

"She really didn't say anything. She didn't like the idea a bit. She was upset at first...I believe because of her love for me, she let me make my own decisions myself. Even though she did not agree with my desires, she just left it between God and me to deal with. She loves me in spite of who I am as a person. She's the best aunt ever. She is my best friend. I can talk to her about anything. She even told me that when I come back to New Orleans that we would go shopping for new clothes."

That night, Rick and Diamond got dressed up and went to the club in their women attire. While they were out at the club, Rick ran into Raymond, his ex-boyfriend, who pulled Rick to the side and said to him, "We need to talk, baby. I miss you."

In Rick's heart, he knew that he was still in love with him. When he saw him, his heart skipped a beat because of the love that lied in the depths of his soul. Diamond knew this, just by looking at Rick's eyes. "Girl, don't do it. That Negro is crazy and no good."

Rick was just standing there. Upon hearing these whispered words, Raymond then grabbed Rick's hands and began to lead him away. At that moment, Diamond said to Rick, "Girl, have you lost your mind?"

Rick turned around and said unto him, "I will be right back."

Raymond looked back at Diamond and rolled his eyes at him. They walked and sat at the bar then Raymond said unto Rick, "Baby, I've been lonely without you ever since you been gone. You are the best thing that has ever happened to me."

Rick said, "If I was the best thing that ever happened to you, why did you beat me the way you did?"

"I was very stressed. I was going through some things at that time in my life, which blinded me from realizing that you are the best thing that ever happened to me. I have changed. I promise I will never put my hands on you ever again. Come back home. I need you."

A few weeks later, Rick moved out of the house with Diamond and moved back with Raymond. They got along great for a couple of months. Everything started to go downhill once Rick found out that Raymond was back to using drugs again. The rage from Raymond's jealous heart caused him to beat Rick again. One night on Rick's way back from the club dressed up in his woman attire, there were a couple of men walking late that night. Once they saw how beautiful he was, they did not know that he was a man.

They grabbed him with the intent to rape him, pushing him against the wall and grabbing him between his legs. Once one of the guys felt his manhood and realized that he was a man, he hollered out to the other two men, "This ain't no women. This a punk a dude!"

Once the other two guys realized what it was that he was saying, they began to beat Rick, kicking on him and stomping on him. Rick cried out as loud as he could say, "Someone please help me."

When one of the guys gave him one last blow to the head, it knocked Rick unconscious. Once the guys noticed that he was unconscious, they went through his purse and took all his money then took off running, leaving him for dead in the dark alley. Fortunately, that same night, there was a man walking late who noticed that there was someone lying in the alley, badly hurt. He decided to walk over to see if this strange lady was hurt, not knowing that she was really a man. He nudged her on the shoulder, saying, "Ma'am, are you okay?"

Rick awoke momentarily and said softly, "Please... help...me..."

The man picked him up and took him to the doctor for help. Once they arrived at the hospital, the doctor treated his critical condition. He stayed there for three months. Once Diamond found out about his accident, she rushed to the hospital to see him. She did not know whether he was going to live or die. She did not call Momma Mamie because he knew Rick didn't want to worry her. When Diamond got to the hospital, he found out that Rick unconscious, lying inside the hospital bed. She just sat by his side, holding his hand, crying and praying that he would wake up talking to him, softly saying, "Girl, it going to be okay. You are going to be just fine. You wait and see." She stayed with Rick for three days until on the third day, Rick miraculously came out of unconsciousness and said unto Diamond, "Hey, girl!"

Diamond, with tears in her eyes, said, "Quiet, baby. Diamond is here."

"Girl, they beat me up really bad."

Diamond didn't know who did this to him. Because Rick was drowsy with medication, he could not tell him who it was who did this to him. In the back of Diamond's mind, she thought that Raymond had done this to him. Within next couple of months, he recovered from his injuries. He was feeling better to the point that he could remember what had happened that night when he left from the club. When Diamond came into the room that morning, Rick was sitting up in the bed. She had some flowers in his hands for him and gave it to him.

Rick said, "Thank you."

"How are you feeling?"

"I'm doing okay. Did you call my Momma Mamie?"

"No."

"Thank you. I didn't want her to know."

"Girl....what happened to you! Who did this to you? I know that no good, good for nothing Negro done this to you."

"No, Raymond did not do this to me. Some guys jumped me and tried to rape me on my way home from the club."

"Do you remember what they looked like?"

"No, not really, but I do remember one of them having a white T-shirt and a white hat. It was so dark when they grabbed from behind. I did not see them."

The next week, Rick was released from the hospital, and Diamond took him home. On their way back to Raymond's house, Diamond said, "Girl, you need to leave that Negro alone because things are just going to get worse between the both of you. That Negro didn't even call or come to see you while you were in the hospital."

Once Rick and Diamond got to Raymond's apartment, Rick rang the doorbell. Raymond came to the door. "Hey, baby! Where have you been?"

He was shocked to see him, as if he did not want him to come in.

Diamond said unto him, "Are you going to let us in? This boy just got out of the hospital."

When they came inside the apartment, another drag queen walked out of the room. "Hey, baby, I could not find the towels."

Diamond opened her mouth with a surprised look on her face. Raymond was caught and did not know what to say.

Rick said unto him, "Who is this swanky-looking bitch up in my house?" His body was not fully healed, but he forgot about the pain that he was in. Rick handed Diamond his bag and ran over to the drag queen and proceeded to beat him in every way.

Diamond dropped the bags. "Beat her ass, girl." Raymond tried to stop them, but Diamond stood in the way and waved her finger in his face and said, "Not today."

Raymond just stood there and knew he had made a big mistake. Once Rick had beat up the drag queen, she grabbed his things and ran out the door. Rick walked up to Raymond and slapped him across the face. "This is the last time you will do this to me! IT's OVER!"

Raymond grabbed Rick's arm. "Baby...Baby...please don't leave. It's not what you think."

"Get your hands off me. Don't you ever touch me again."

As Rick walked out the door, Diamond turned her head at Raymond and rolled her eyes at him and slammed the door behind them. While they were in the car, Rick was very hurt, mad, with tears falling from his eyes.

"Girl, you did that!" Diamond said, with excitement on her face.

Even though Rick's body healed, his heart was still broken inside. At this point in his life, he knew he had to do something different with his life. There was one thing that he knew he had to do, and that was move to out of Miami so he could get a new start. When Rick lay in bed that night, he thought about change. He knew that Momma Mamie had an answer for him. He decided to call her. Joe answered the phone, and he automatically knew who he was and was very excited to hear from him.

Rick said, "How are you doing?"

Joe replied, "Fine, son. It has been a long time since we heard from you. The madam has been worrying about..."

"I know...where is she? May I speak to her?"

"One minute."

Once Momma Mamie made it to the phone, she said, "How are you doing, child? It's good to hear from you. Where have you been, child? I have been worried sick about you. Is everything all right?"

"Everything is fine, Momma."

"When are you coming down to see your old Momma Mamie?"

"Soon. I do not know when. I have decided to move to Atlanta, Georgia."

"Child, why? Is everything all right?"

"Everything is fine. I feel that I need to move to a new area so that I can get my thoughts together."

"You know you cannot pull the wool over my eyes. I tell you what, before you make that decision, why won't you come back to New Orleans? We just hired a new preacher. We are getting ready to start our annual revival this week. Child, this revival might just be the thing you need that will help you get yourself together."

"I know, Momma, but I just need time for myself."

"Child, have your Momma Mamie ever stirred you wrong?"

"No, Momma, no."

"I will come. I will be there tomorrow."

At this point in his life, he had decided that he would totally live his life as a woman and become the next madam who would supersede the legacy of Momma Bea. He knew that his life was at its end, and there was something missing inside his cold heart. He just did not know what it was. He thought to himself that Momma Mamie might be right; maybe the church thing might be the thing that he needs to turn things around. He hoped that the words that Momma Mamie said unto him and this church revival would give him the answers he was looking for.

Chapter 13

Once he arrived at the airport, Momma Mamie and Joe were standing, waiting for him with Pussy Wussy, her beloved Scottish Terrier dog. As Rick approached, Joe didn't know who he was. When Momma Mamie saw him, she automatically knew who he was. When he got closer, he said unto them, "Momma Mamie, it's me, Rick!"

Joe gave Rick a look as if he said to himself, *I have seen many things in my life, but I had never seen a man change himself into a woman.* He just stood there with his mouth wide open in disbelief.

Momma Mamie said unto him, "You look beautiful… you look like your Momma Ernestine."

She gave him a big hug, knowing in the back of her mind that it hurt her to see Rick change his life the way he did. *Will the next madam come now that Rick's desire is to be like that of a woman?* Despite Rick's decision, she accepted him for who he was as a person and not for what he had become. Once they got back to the mansion that afternoon, Lady, the maid, had prepared a dinner for them. Momma Mamie said unto Rick, "Child, it's good to see you. Look at you, looking all beautiful. Child, I have seen many things, but honey, I have not seen nothing like this. Baby, you make a beautiful madam. Tell me, child, how has life been treating you?"

At that moment, Rick began to cry. "Not so good, Momma. I am unhappy."

"Child, what is wrong? Do not cry, child. Everything going to be just fine."

"My heart is broken into pieces, Momma. I feel like I'm all alone. It seems that everyone I have been with, I have loved with all my heart, have used me for what it is that I have, not for the beauty that lied with in me. Sometimes I say to myself, what is the use of living if you say to your heart that you love someone and they are not willing to love you back? What is the use, Momma, what is the use?"

"I know how it is that you feel. I believe, hon, that the reason so many people hearts are broken from the desire of love, they try searching for love in the wrong place and in the wrong ways, and until one start searching for love in the way that God has intended for a man and a women to find it, he nor she will every find happiness."

Rick continued crying. "Momma, I know God's plan for women and man. Tell me the reason, why is it that my heart tells me that it is my destiny to love a man, not a woman?"

"Child, the devil has many tricks up his sleeve, and he has played a trick on your heart, son."

She put her arms around him. "In order for a person to find true love, he first must find a friendship with God, then first love himself before he can love someone else and expect someone to clearly see how to love him. You have to love yourself, child, before someone else can love you. If you are listening to the words in which I have spoken unto you, child, and take heed one day, you will find the person of your dream to love. You just have to be patient, and it will come. Child, you know it was not easy for your old Momma Mamie before I found my darling Earl. A long time ago, I felt the same way you do. Once upon a time, when I was courting, it took me a long time to find my true love, baby. I tell you that I had some no good Negroes in my lifetime. Through the storm, I prayed to the good Lord above, and he blessed me with my darling Earl. Baby, I knew I was in love from the moment I first saw him. He was a young good-looking man of God. All the women in the church wanted him. When I walked into the church house, I let them have, baby, I was not going to let anything stop me from getting my man. There was one woman named Evelyn who was dating him at the time. Baby, I did not even let her stop me from getting what it was that I wanted because I knew I had everything he needed in women. When I saw him first time, I looked in his eyes. He knew at that moment what he had to do for me for a lifetime." Momma Mamie gazed at the ceiling. "He had been doing just that ever since, until the good Lord took him far from my heart. You see, child, when you find the one who will love you for life, baby honey child, he will know what it takes to make you smile until the very hair on your hair turns gray."

"When, Momma?"

Momma Mamie said, thinking of Uncle Pittman, as if her breath had been taken away, "Soon, child, real soon!"

From hearing the words spoken by Momma Mamie, Rick gained hope, thinking that there is somebody out there who could love him the way he needed to be loved.

"Child, as beautiful as you are, you just a fingertip away from the touch of love. When you find it, don't let anything keep you away from it, because it is yours to have." Momma Mamie then hugged him tighter. "Child, in time, everything will be just fine."

The next morning, she and Rick had breakfast out on the back deck of the mansion. She said unto him, "Child, you need a new hairdo. I need to go to the beauty shop this afternoon so I can look good for the revival, and I am going to take you with me. I will introduce you as my niece. What shall I call you?"

"Just call me Madam Colleen."

That afternoon, Momma Mamie took Rick to her private hair salon and introduced him as her niece Madam Colleen. After he got his hair fixed by the hairdresser, the hairdresser handed him the mirror so he could see his new hairdo. When he looked in the mirror, he was amazed about how well his hair was done—he looked like a princess going to a ball. They then went to Momma Mamie's designer to find something to wear for the revival; they both tried on some beautiful hats and dresses from the wall inside the dress shop. After shopping that afternoon, they went to one of Momma Mamie's favorite restaurants. They sat out on the outdoor dining area to eat lunch. As Rick sat down on his chair, Momma Mamie noticed that he did not sit down like a lady should sit herself. She then said, "Child, you have a whole lot to learn when it comes to being a lady. It looks like I will have to teach you a couple of old tricks that will allow you to shine above all the other ladies in the chicken coup."

After eating lunch, Momma Mamie told Joe to go and get the car. The next day, she showed Rick the proper ways of being a lady, things like how to hold up the perfect posture in walking like a lady. "Baby, one thing to always remember, a true lady never lets her anger be seen. She holds it in as a smile but gets her point across with never letting anyone know how mad she really is." She had him practice walking across the floor with a book on his head while she sat in her chair. Joe walked pass them, where they were practicing; he shook his head and walked off. That afternoon was the start of the revival.

Chapter 14

Once they arrived at the church, and walked through the doors, everyone stood because of the respect that they had for Momma Mamie in being the first lady of the church, since the new preacher did not have a wife. The usher led them down the aisle as if they were royalty; the people in the church started to stare at Rick, wondering because they had never seen her before, *Who is this woman who walks with Momma Mamie?* They were then seated in front of the church where Momma Mamie had been sitting for thirty years. As the lead singer sang, it put Rick into another world because of the beautiful melody that flowed from the young woman's soul to GOD before the new preacher came out to the pulpit. On the last hymn of the song, the elders and deacons sitting in the pulpit stood and told the church to stand as the preacher walked to the pulpit. The choir began to sing "Amazing Grace." The woman who led the song had a voice like that of thunder. The preacher came out with the excitement of the Holy Ghost in his soul; he had a voice like that of a rushing wind. At that moment, when Rick saw him, his heart began to melt for the spirit. Rick then leaned over to Momma Mamie and asked her, "Where is his wife?"

She then said. "He did not have one." She noticed Rick staring at the preacher, not concerned about his sermon. "Child, don't you even think about it. My Lord, he is a MAN OF GOD!" She began fanning her face. After the service was over, as they walked toward the back doors of the church, the preacher was standing, shaking the church members' hands as they exited the church. As Rick approach him, his heart was rushing as if it was a thousand horses running across a lonely desert in search for water. Rick stared into his eyes, and in return, he then noticed him and stared in his eyes too. Rick gave him a look, the look that let him know that he believed in the depths of his soul, that you are the one that my soul had yearned for from the day of my birth. The preacher then gave Rick the look that he knew what to do to him for the rest of his life, that he was really man, not a woman. The preacher gave him that look, as if he could make him smile until his hair turned gray. Once Rick touched his hand to give him a handshake, he felt as if he didn't want to let go of the preacher then tilted his head in homage, saying unto him, "Hello, my dear lady"—he kissed her hand—"may I ask you your name?"

Rick said, "You can call me Madam Colleen."

Momma Mamie was standing on the other side of Rick, thinking to herself, *This boy has lost his mind.*

He then said, "My name is John Austin."

Momma Mamie said, standing with a look on her face, "Yes, baby, this is my niece from Miami, Florida. Lord help her soul. She's going to be staying for a few weeks with me."

Reverend John said unto Rick, "That great!" He looked at him in his eyes. "Maybe you can show me around New Orleans."

Before Rick could respond, Momma Mamie said, "I don't thank...Colleen...will be able to do that. She's going to be quite busy during her stay here...right, Colleen?"

He totally ignored Momma Mamie words. "I think I could make a little time for the preacher, Momma Mamie."

Momma Mamie then opened her mouth wide because she couldn't believe that Rick was actually considering going out with a *man of god*. It just ran her hot.

Reverend John said, "Great, it's a date! Here is my number. Give me a call when you find time in you busy schedule."

Momma Mamie and Rick left the church. As they walked to the car, Momma Mamie looked at Rick as if he had lost his mind. Once they got into the car, Momma Mamie said unto Rick, "Boy, have you lost your mind! That man doesn't know that you are really a man. I will not stand for it! Do you hear me, child?"

"Oh, Momma, it is nothing...I am just showing him around the town. What harm could come out of it? Who knows maybe he'll give me the spiritual guidance I need that would make me a better Christian."

Momma Mamie rolled her eyes. "Baby, I am warning you. I do not want you to get your heart broken." She then looked out the window and stared outside, looking upset. Rick had the biggest smile on his face, as if he was in another world of his own.

The next day, Rick called Reverend John. He was a young, good-looking man. Once he answered the phone, he was surprised to hear from Rick. "It's good to hear from you so soon."

Rick said, "I am very excited about taking you out on the town so you can see what New Orleans has to offer."

"I have also looked forward in you talking me out on that venture. When would be a good time for us to take that venture?"

"Lets say noon-ish on tomorrow."

"Great! I'll be there at twelve o'clock sharp to pick you up."

After Rick hung up that phone with him, calmness filled the depths of his empty soul. The next morning when she awoke, as he put on his woman attire, she looked in the mirror, brushing her hair. He asked himself the question, *Could it be that I have found someone who could make me smile until my hair grows gray?*

Something inside him answered the question that was lingered, saying unto him, *Yes, I think you have found that person.* He began to sing a hymn as he stroked the gold satin brush through his long beautiful hair, staring in a daze. Once he got dressed, he went downstairs to have breakfast with Momma Mamie. She was of course sitting, drinking coffee, reading the newspaper, checking on the status of her oil company, still disturbed by Rick's response to Reverend John from the night before. Rick was filled with happiness and the emotional drive that lied in the midst of his blissful heart, as he got downstairs to the dining quarters. Blinded by the desire of his heart, he began to feel connection with Reverend John against the spiritual arena in which he dwelled. Momma Mamie saw the excitement that ran across his face. Once he sat down at the table, Momma Mamie said to him with a suspicious look on her face, "Child, what are you up to?"

Rick arose from his chair and walked toward the food table. "Oh, I am going out with a preacher today...Reverend John. He and I have an engagement in seeing the city of New Orleans."

Momma Mamie's blood began to rush within her veins. With a loud voice, she said unto him, "Child! Have you lost...your...MIND! You can't be possibly considering going out with that MAN! Have you forgotten who you are, child? You are gust looking for trouble?"

"Momma, need not to worry. This is innocent. I do not see anything wrong with hang out with someone who could possibly help me become spiritually strong. Momma, is it that why you asked me to come here to do?"

"Yes, child, that's what I wanted, but you have something else on you mind, and it ain't no spiritual healing. Child, don't' you know I saw how you were looking at that man the other night at that church house and how you were holding his hand, staring in to his eyes with lust written all over your face. Baby honey, you better tell that to someone else because I was not born yesterday. You got to get pretty early in the morning to pull the wool over this old hen. What if that man finds out that you are really a man and not a woman? Do you know, child, the embarrassment that it would bring on the church and this family? Think about what it is that you are doing, child. Baby honey, listen to me, I love you with all my heart. Don't let the fire of lust in your eyes broke you, child. You are all I got. It's enough that I have accepted what it is that you have done to your body, transforming yourself from the person that God has created you to be. Ask me, child, why it is that I have allowed you to come into this house with this great sin. It is because I cannot stand the fact of you getting out in this profane society of ours and letting the curse of the madam taking the breath of life out of your soul. It is my hope, child, that you change your ways before God call your name. I'm not going to try and stop you from whatever it is that your heart desire, because you know right from wrong. In spite of your mistakes and wrongdoings, I still love you. I tell you one thing, and I want you to listen to me real good, child. When you go out with that man, you better know who it is that you are dealing with and respect that because the man you are dealing with is not just an ordinary man—he is a man of God. Now you go and get the spiritual heal that you have come here for and come back home, leaving that man heart where it's at. Do you hear me, child? Because if you do not, God is going to whip you every which way but lose." Once Momma Mamie spoke those words unto Rick, he walked off, saddened from his hidden desires. Because of the desires of Rick's heart, the words of Momma Mamie went in one ear and out the other.

Chapter 15

Once twelve o'clock came around, Rick was upstairs fleshing up at that time. Reverend John rang the doorbell, and Joe answered the door and let him inside. "Reverend John Adams has arrived. Right this way."

Once Rick heard the announcement, his heart began to beat fast as he hurried in getting ready. Rick came of out the room and stood on top of the stairway, looking down into Sir John's eyes in amazement. When he saw him dressed so beautifully, John looked up into his eyes as if he had seen the queen of the Nile. Rick had on a beautiful white dress with matching gloves and hat. At that moment, Momma Mamie walked inside the room where Reverend John was standing at the bottom of the stairway. He didn't even notice that she was there standing beside him; he was amazed with Rick's beauty. His eyes were stuck on him because he was so beautiful to her, thinking to herself that he was up to something that was not good. Once he reached the bottom of the stairway, Reverend John grabbed his hand and kissed it. "My Madam Colleen, I must tell you that you are beautiful."

He said, "Thank you, my handsome man."

Momma Mamie stood off into the background, looking amazing, with disgrace across her face. As they walked to the car, it was if Rick had gotten weak within himself. His heart spoke to him, as he looked at John from the side, *Could it be that this man could love me for a lifetime?* Once they reached the car, Reverend John opened the car door and let Rick inside.

Reverend John then said as they were riding, "Madam Colleen, if I may, could I ask you a question?"

Rick began to tremble within himself. "You may."

"How are it that you are so beautiful?"

"It is a gift that has been given to me from the good Lord from above."

"I can truly say that he has giving you the most precious gift that has been seen within the eyes of the world." John then asked, "Where are we going to today?"

"I thought we would go out and eat lunch at one of me and Momma Mamie's favorite restaurants, then we can go to one of New Orleans's finest highlights."

Once they got to the restaurant, the waitresses seated them outside, on the back deck for the upper class blacks of the restaurant. Once they were seated John said unto him, "This is a really nice restaurant."

"I come here all the time. I am glad you like it."

"So tell me, what brings you to New Orleans?"

"By it being that I am Momma Mamie's only living niece, once I heard that Uncle Pittman had pasted away, I decided to come and visit her to see how she was doing and also help her with the family business that he left for us to take care."

"It's the funniest thing that Madam Mamie had never spoke you before."

"Maybe she never had a chance to, by it being that I have been gone for a long time." "Where do you live?"

"I live in Miami, Florida. Unfortunately, I will be moving to Atlanta, Georgia. Enough about me. Tell me about me about you."

"Well, I was raised in Montgomery Alabama in a small three-bedroom house with my grandmother, grandfather, and mother with my three bothers and sisters. My father was not around much."

"Are they still living?"

"My father is not, but my mother is. She still lives in the same old house that my grandparents used to stay in. Is your mother still living?

"No she is not. She had died when I was a small child. After her death, I moved in with Momma Mamie. She raised me. When I got old enough, she sent me to a private school for girls. I stayed there most of my childhood until I graduated high school. After that, I moved away for college."

"Enough about the history of your life. Let's focus on the history of our minds, my lady. So tell me, what activities are you active in, and what is it that you love doing?"

"I am not involved with anyone at this time. I am waiting for the right encounter to come my way."

"How will you know if he is the right one when he comes your way?"

"That easy? Thinking in the back of him mind, I have already found him. He just doesn't know it yet," he said, reflecting back on the night when his eyes connected with his. He remembered a conversation he had with Momma Mamie on how she knew she had found the love of her life, Uncle Pittman. How she knew he was the one for her. Momma Mamie told him his uncle looked into her eyes and instantly knew what it took to make her smile for a lifetime, until every hair on her head turns gray.

Reverend John then said, as he looked into his eyes, amazed with her beauty, "One day, you will soon find the right one."

"Yes, one day, yes…real soon, I will." His broken heart told him that he had already found the man who will be able to make him smile until the very hair on his head turns gray.

"So tell me, what you like to do for fun?"

"I like a lot of things like reading poetry, prose precious, and singing in my spare time."

"So you like to sing."

"Yes, I do well."

"Well, I like to sing a little myself. I have been singing since I was a small child in my grandmother's church choir."

"That's a fine thing. I first started sing when I moved in with my Momma Mamie in the Mount Zion church choir as a small child before the death of my mother."

"You know, the Lord can really use you if you at Mount Zion if you ever to decide to stay here in New Orleans."

"You know, you are right, who knows he might just make that happen."

They then began to smile as they both looked into each other's eyes.

Rick said, "So tell me some, Reverend John, how did you become a very powerful preacher?"

"Call me Johnny. That's what my grandfather used to call me when he was living."

"It is a privilege for me to call you John, something your grandfather called you."

"You asked me the question how did I become the preacher that I am? As a young boy, I always wanted to become a preacher due to the influence giving to my by my grandmother and God. She would always tell me that 'One of these days you are going to be one of the greatest preachers who ever lived.'That's what inspired me to become a preacher. So tell me how it was in your boarding school?"

"It was all right. I had everything that a child would dream of having. The only thing that was challenging was missing my mother holding me every night. Once I finished boarding school, Momma Mamie sent me to Moore House University. Once I finished college, I received a degree in business management and marketing. I then began to work at R&B Oil Company for Momma Mamie as president. When Uncle Pittman died, he left me half of the company."

"How were you able to work at the company and live in Miami?"

"My Momma Mamie and Uncle Pittman hired a CEO by the name of Jiffery to run the company. He has been doing a great job. He runs the company for us. He sends me monthly reports on the status of the company each month. Once I received them, I looked them over and sent him memos. So that's how I dealt with the company."

"My, you are a very busy lady."

"That I am, that I am."

After eating dinner, they decided to take a walk through the park. As they were walking, Rick then asked him, "So tell me, who am your favorite poet?"

"Robert Frost. From reading his work, it has helped me realize the true meaning of what love is."

"Any particular poem?"

"Why, yes. The one that I loved above all is entitled 'Devotion.' It really helped me to see what love really is. The quote 'The heart can think no devotion greater than being shore to an ocean, holding a curve of one position, counting on endless repetition.'"

"Lady Madam, from hearing those words that I have convey unto you, what is it that you gather from the flowing stream of this poet's heart?

"My dear sir, I have a lost for word from hearing this great melody of beautiful words. My dear man, please tell me what is your heart speaks of from hearing those words of this great poet."

"When I think of this great piece, my heart tells me that when Robert Frost wrote this poem, he either experienced are knew someone knew of this type of love or stood in front of a great ocean where it enabling him to dig deep within himself to find the words he needed to express himself about the one true love that passes all understanding. For some strange reason, I envisioned him sitting by a shore of an ocean in the late afternoon of the day. In other words, the world-renowned writer of beautiful words paints a portrait of what love is. He goes on to say the heart can't think of no devotion greater than being shown the ocean. He compares the emotions of the heart to the width and depth of that of an ocean, meaning that the love that flows from the rivers of the heart is great. This statement helped the reader to see the emotional desire of his heart when it comes to genuine love is wide and deep like that of a great ocean. When a person loves another, the mind can no longer fathom it. Have you ever stood and looked out over a great ocean?"

"Yes, I have. When I looked out over it, it appeared that the ocean has no end to it, as if it ran right into the sky." From hearing these words spoken by John, Rick was amazed by the rhythm of his voice and the flow of words he used to express his ideas on the poetry of Robert Frost's poem.

John went on to say as Robert Frost continued to explore his heart, "The bay of the ocean stands as the expression of adversity that arises in the relationship between two people. The endless reputation that Robert Frost speaks of in this peace represent the waves that flow from the heart of the sea when you stand out over the bay and look out over the water of the sea or ocean. Once the waves hit against the bay, it appears as if they stop momentarily but are resented as continuing rolling. That how the waves of love roll from the heart of the soul of the person who is presented loves another regardless of how a person makes you mad, or whatever mistakes of which you love make the wave of the heart love you in spite of whatever. One day, madam, I hope to find that treasure of love in someone."

At that moment, Rick felt in his heart that John was the one that he had been waiting for all his life. John had given Rick strength; he had shined a light of hope into the darkest places of Rick's heart for the first time of his life. After hearing these words spoken by John, all Rick could say was, "Me too, my darling, me too."

As they continued to walk, they stared into each other's eyes, as if they knew they would be together for a lifetime. Knowing the ocean of love that lied inside their hearts, neither one of them could ever drink it all in one lifetime. After walking, they went to see some more beautiful sights of the city, and Reverend John then dropped Rick back at home. Once they got to Momma Mamie's house, Reverend

John got out of the car while Rick sat and waited until he opened his door for him to exit out. Once he got to the door on the other side of the car, he reached inside his pocket inside his suit and pulled out a handkerchief and placed it on the ground for him to step out on it. He then opened the door and grabbed Rick's hand and helped him out of the car; he walked him to the front door of his house.

Reverend John then said unto him, kissing the back of Rick's hand, "Madam Colleen, it has been a great reward for me today spending the time that I have spent with you today.

"It too has been a great experience I have had with you too."

"We must do it again real soon."

"We must."

Reverend John then kissed him on his cheek. "I will be calling you real soon."

"I will be waiting. Good afternoon, my handsome gentleman."

Chapter 16

O nce Rick entered the house, Momma Mamie was sitting there, waiting, hoping in her little soul that he had not done anything that went against God and hoping that he would not get himself caught up with something that would cause him hurt and pain.

When Rick entered the room, Momma Mamie said unto him, "Child, have a seat." As Rick sat down, his heart began rushing like that of a rushing wind, but joy filled his heart from the outing spent with Reverend John. Once he was seated, Momma Mamie said, "So, child, how was your outing with the reverend?"

Rick said, "It was great. He is a very sweet and *godly* man."

"I hope that in every ounce of blood in me that you don't try to love on that man of God. Baby honey child, you are playing with fire. I see something in your eyes I have never seen before. I hope for your sake and mind that what I am think isn't lying in your heart. Change your heart, child, because the Lord in heaven is sitting high and he is looking low at what it is that you are doing and he is not pleased. I am not trying to tell you how to live your life because I know you have to live with your own decision. I just do not want you to be hurt, child. I have seen many things in my life, child, but this is the first time I have seen something like this." Momma Mamie grabbed his hand. "Child, you are so beautiful, and you have a good heart. What I am trying to tell you, child, is, protect your heart, child, and do not continue leading that man on.

Joe was done preparing their meal. "Dinner is ready.

Momma Mamie rose out of her chair to head toward the quarters. "Hear the wind of wisdom, child."

Rick sat down and thought about her words, but the lust of his heart kept the flow with his desire for Reverend John. Once Momma Mamie got to the doors of the study, she said, "Child, are you going to eat with your old Momma Mamie?"

"Yes, Momma, I'm coming. Just give me a minute."

Once they got inside the dining quarters and began eating, it was very quiet for a moment them. Momma Mamie said, "Child, tomorrow I'll be having the ladies' monthly meeting here at the mansion, and I want you to come so the other women can meet you as my niece, child."

"What should I wear?"

"Dress like a lady and wear a hat and some gloves the best inside your closet. It will take place at two o'clock sharp when you and I will open the doors of the mansion. Please be downstairs on time. Please, child, we do not what to keep the ladies waiting. This will be very important moment for the legacy of the Madam Momma Bea. May she rest in piece. From this point on, since I am not going to be around forever in time, I will be turning the keys of our legacy over to you, child, since there is no other seed left but you. It is my pray that you change your life, baby honey child, and give us a madam that will supersede our legacy, child. There is one more thing I have to tell you, child, if you are going to represent the madam that will supersede the legacy of Momma Bea, baby honey child, I want you to be the best lady that you can be, like that of your Momma Mamie. After I am gone, you will take over the house, the oil company, and the ladies' organization that you will be attending tomorrow, so, child, be on your best behavior because they are going to be watching you to see if you got what it takes to be their leader."

"Momma, I wont let you down."

Momma Mamie then kissed him on his forehead. "I know, child." And then she head to her room for her afternoon nap.

The next morning, Momma Mamie and Rick had their breakfast. Momma Mamie said, "Child, is you ready to meet the other women in the ladies meeting today?"

Rick said, "I am more ready the ever."

While eating breakfast, Joe came into the dining quarters. "Madam Colleen, you have a phone call. Would you like to take it in here?"

Rick said, "No, I will take it in the other room." He then removed himself from his seat. "Excuse me." Once he got to the phone, it was Reverend John. Upon hearing his voice on the other end of the phone, a chill ran through his soul.

Reverend John said, "How are you doing? I'm sorry I am calling you so early in the morning."

Rick said, "Oh, it's all right. I have been waiting on your call."

"The reason for my call is that I wanted to ask you out for dinner this afternoon."

"How nice of you. I am sorry, but I can not go today because I have a ladies' meeting with Momma Mamie and our guest here at the house. Maybe tomorrow we could have a picnic somewhere."

"That would be great. What about tomorrow afternoon around four o'clock?"

"That would be great. I will make some sandwiches, and you get some wine. I know the ideal place at the county park right in front of the river."

"I think that's a great idea. I will be there at three thirty sharp."

"That's a date, my handsome gentleman." Once he hung up the phone with Reverend John, he went back into the dining quarters to finish eating breakfast with Momma Mamie. Once he took his seat at the breakfast table, he had a smile on his face and joy in his heart.

Momma Mamie said, "Child, who was that on the phone?"

Rick could not lie to her. "That was Reverend John calling to ask me out to eat dinner."

"Well what did you say?

"I told him that I would be able to go with him to day because we had our lady meeting today, but we could hang out tomorrow afternoon for a picnic out on the river. Don't worry, Momma, everything is going to be okay. It is innocent."

"Child, did not I tell you that you are playing with fire? You are just looking for trouble. Must I remind you that you are a man and not a woman? Okay, child, that's your life. I still love you anyways, but remember when it comes back to hunt you, just remember I told you so. Now, child, go and start getting yourself ready for your meeting time is passing. The ladies will be here soon."

When two o'clock came around, Momma Mamie was standing at the door of the mansion, holding Pussy Wussy, her dog Scottish territory, with Rick standing right beside her. Once the grandfather clock went off, Momma Mamie gave Joe the signal to open the door and let the ladies inside. Momma Mamie introduced Rick as her niece; Rick greeted them with a smile, and he handled it really well. Once everyone came in and was seated in the living room area, they all sat down and had tea after their tea session ended. Momma Mamie arose from her seat with a teacup in her hand and began the tap on it, saying unto the guests inside the room, "It is time for our monthly meeting to start, ladies." She approached the speaking stand, hitting her teacup, calling the meeting into order. She then went on to say once she got behind the podium, "It is great for you all to be here on this lovely day. As all of you know, my niece has been here in New Orleans to helping me out. As you all know that I am not going to be around forever even though my beauty wants to go on for ever." Everyone inside the room laughed. "After I am gone, I want to leave the seat of chairman to the next seed of the madam, my niece Madam Colleen."

Momma Mamie then asked Rick to come up to the podium. Everyone applauded. "If she proves herself worthy, it is my prayer that you would grant my request."

Everyone clapped their hands with acceptance, welcoming him as a new member, not knowing his secret of being a man.

Chapter 17

The next day, Rick and Reverend John went on a picnic. He arrived at Rick's house at three thirty o'clock sharp that afternoon. Rick had prepared sandwiches in a beautiful picnic basket he borrowed from Momma Mamie. Once John opened the car door and let Rick inside, they drove off to the river for the picnic. Once they got to the riverside, John opened the door for him. He then opened the trunk of the car and got out some wine glasses and the basket with a bottle of wine. He also pulled out a book from one of his favorite authors. Once they found their spot, he then laid down a blanket and began pouring the both of them wine in each of their glasses.

As Rick sat down on the blanket, John said unto him, "My, you are the most beautifulness woman my eyes had ever seen." John then pulled out one of his favorite novels by William James, who expressed his thoughts on what reality is. John said unto Rick, "The other day, I was reading this book. in it I read something that really touched me within, and I wanted to share it with you. I wanted to see what you think about it."

Rick then said in his lady voice, "Please share it with me."

John then opened the book and found the place where he had marked the peace that stirred his soul. He then began reading the words of William James, "Anything that exceeds forever, escapes statement withdraw from definition, must be glimpsed and felt not told.

In hearing these words spoken by John, Rick became speechless, with no response to give. John then asked Rick, who was dressed in his beautiful woman attire, "What is it that you had gathered from the words that you heard from his great poet?"

Rick could do nothing but smile, with his tongue relaxed. With no response at that moment, John began to covey his thoughts on what he thought the author was trying to express in this piece. "I believe that William James in this piece expresses the unanswered questions of the dwelling of reality. In other words, what he is saying is that there are certain things in the existence of the life of an individual that the human tongue cannot speak on and the Webster's dictionary cannot define what it is. The human sense touch and the human eye sees cannot express what it the sees with words or definition. He or she can only look at it or feel it to know that it exist. For example, if someone were to ask you to define the aroma of coffee, could you give them a definition without using a synonym of the term? Or if someone were asked you the define silences, could you define it? One philosopher said the best way to define silence, is to stand the middle of a wilderness when the oak tree is standing still and the wind is now blowing then you shall find the definition of silence. You can only see with your eyes and feel the presence of silence with the senses giving to you by God and not give a definition of what it is. This is just how the wind of silence is blowing through the nostrils of my heart. This wind of which I speak of is the wind of love it's speaking to the realm of my soul. The words of which it speaks, it withdrawals from definition and escapes the statement of my tongue. When it comes time for me to express what it is that I feel, when I look into your eyes, Madam Colleen, it is if I am looking into the eyes of a white dove, so pure, so white. That the definitions that had entered into the parts of my soul had left me speechless."

As Rick looked into his eyes, John grabbed his hand. At that moment, Rick felt as if the undefined words in John's heart were as clear as night and day. As Rick continued to look into John's eyes, from speaking these words unto him, he believed that John would be able to love him for a lifetime and bring light to the most darkest parts of his soul and help him to answer the unanswered questions that lied in the back of his mind—if only he would give him a chance to do so. At that moment, Rick felt that same wind of love that rushed through the capillaries of John's heart. They then arose up from the blanket in which they were sitting and held hands as they walked under the southern trees of New Orleans, along the riverside. The wind blew across their face, with their minds relaxed as they took a great journey through each other's minds, filled with emotion and passion to a place, taking Rick places he had never been before.

At that moment, Rick forgot all his problems—in the past and in the present. For the first time in his life, he believed that he had finally found someone to love and someone who could really love him back.

Chapter 18

The next morning when Rick awoke, he woke up with joy all over his face, forgetting about who he was as a man and the great problems that could possibly hinder him from loving John for a lifetime. Once he got dressed, he walked downstairs into the dining area, to eat breakfast, humming to himself. Momma Mamie at that time was sitting, eating her breakfast and drinking a cup of coffee. Rick was overwhelmed in his mind, thinking about the lovely time he and John shared on the evening before and how much John made him feel great about himself. He was so caught up in his rim of happiness he did not even notice that Momma Mamie was sitting inside the dining quarters.

Momma Mamie said unto him in a suspicious tone, "My, aren't you in a good mood this morning, child. Where is all this excitement coming from?"

Rick then said to her, "It is a beautiful day to be a lady. That's all, Momma."

"Child, have you still been seeing that boy? I hope you are not leading that man on. Listen to me, child, and you listen well. You are playing with fire. What if this man finds out that you are a man and not a woman? Tell me, child, just what will you do?"

"He's not going to find out. Momma, did not you tell me once, if you want something, don't let nothing and no one stand in your way of getting it?"

"Child, have you lost your ever lasting mind! This is a man of God for Christ sake you are lusting after. The good Lord above is not pleased on how you are carrying yourself chasing after this man. It's enough, child. You have come here dressed like a woman. Now you trying to take a man of God down." Momma Mamie then took a deep breath and calmed herself down. "Baby honey child, don't think I'm trying chastened you. I just don't want your heart to be broken, child, because of this great big desire of lust that lies in your heart for this man."

"But, Momma, it's not lust that I am feeling. This man makes me happy. When we hang out, it's as if the melodies of his heart speak to me in ways I have never heard before. It makes my very soul feel at peace. If it is wrong before God the way I feel, I do not what no part of the spirit of God."

"Child, hush your mouth. Do you knew what it is that you are saying?"

"Momma, I have never been as happy as I am now in my whole life."

"Child, this is not an ordinary man that we are talking about. He is a preacher, a man of God. What do you think he would do you if he finds out about your state, child?"

Rick stood speechless. Momma Mamie went on to say, as tears fell from her eyes, "Baby honey child, listen to me and listen to me good. Take care of your soul because in the end, that's all you have left." At that moment, Rick did not know what she meant by that statement, but in time, he will soon find out.

Momma Mamie continued, "I am just trying to protect your from heart, baby, that all and the curse of the madam. If something should happen to you, my little heart could not take it. It would just break me into peace. Do you hear me, child? You must stop see him, child, so you will save me a lot of hurt and yourself a lot of pain. Child, have I ever told you anything wrong?

"No, Momma." Rick cried from the thought of letting the love of his life go. Momma Mamie had convinced him to do so. He then said, "Okay, Momma, I will be leaving tomorrow, and I will forget that I ever knew him."

"Good, child, it will be the best thing for you to do. Believe me, baby, this is the right thing to do."

Before Rick left that morning, he called John. "John, it's me Colleen. I have something to tell you. I will be leaving the first thing in the morning for Miami."

John then asked him, "Why so soon? Is everything okay?"

"I have some business that I have to take care of."

"Well, can we have lunch before you go?"

"I do not think that will be a good idea. Besides, my plane is leaving shortly."

"Is everything okay?"

Rick cried on the phone. "I just think it will be best we never see each other ever again."

"Why, Madam Colleen? Was it something I done or said?"

"It's just best. I am sorry. Good-bye, John."

He then hung up the phone. That morning when Rick left out on the plane, his spirit of love was broken. As he looked out the window of the airplane, tears began to fall from his eyes. He thought to himself, *If only God made me into a woman, I could be with the man of my dreams.* He then cried even more and wiped the tears from his eyes with a bored-pattern handkerchief from his Momma Mamie.

Chapter 19

Once he arrived in Miami at Diamond's apartment, Rick found Diamond sitting down in her room, doing her makeup in front of the mirror. While she was looking in the mirror, she noticed Rick standing behind him, inside the door with his bags in his hand, with tears running down his face.

Diamond then turned around and said, "Baby, was wrong? Don't tell me you ran into that no count Negro again?

Rick said, "No, Diamond, I am in love."

"Well, child, if being in love make you feel like that, I don't want no parts of it."

"This is not the time to be making jokes, Diamond. I am serious. I am really in love. My heart has been broken."

"Okay, baby, pay me no mind. I do not understand. If you are in love, how it that your heart is broken?"

"It happen during my trip in New Orleans, visiting Momma Mamie. I went to a revival at her church to meet their new preacher, and that's when I meet him, the man of my dream."

"Who, girl?"

"The preacher."

"Girl, have you lost your mind? The preacher!"

"I knew it's a bit extreme, but he makes me fell in ways I have never felt before. Girl, he loves me, and I love him. I mean once he became a part of my life, he has taken my mind in places far beyond the stars in the heavens."

"Well, if this man is perfect like you say he is, what is the problem? Don't tell me he found out you were a man."

"No, he does not know."

"Girl, have you thought about what it is that you are doing? What if he find out about you then what will you do?"

"I don't care anything about that now, girl. I just want to love. All my life, I wanted a chance to just love someone once in my life, and they love me back for me. Now that I have the opportunity to love someone with ever effort inside of me. Girl, you know better than anyone else, how bad I have been beat and hurt in my pass relationship. Momma Mamie, with her old traditional beliefs, comes now and tells me, I must stop loving him because it is wrong in the eyesight of God. I know she do not want me to be hurt and disappointed, and I believe what she is telling me is right. Tell me something, Diamond, if it is so wrong, why is it that my heart has been beaten like a drum, day after day, from the very moment our eyes connected? I do not know, Diamond. I just do not know with every ounce of thought inside me why it is so wrong for two people to just love. Why is that so wrong? If there is a God, cannot he see the hurt that I have endured in trying to love so many who did not know how to love me? I mean, can he not see the sincerity that lies inside my heart to love this man with all of my heart? Oh, I don't know anymore what to do, but there is one thing that I do know for sure, is that the hurt that burns around my heart hurts so bad that at times I feel like cutting the very vein that causes the blood of love to flow through it. This feeling that I have inside me for him hurts so bad, Diamond. I mean to know with every inch of my soul that I have met the man of my dreams who can really love me for who it is that dwells inside this unwanted body that I am imprison in. It's like a dream come true, girl, to know and feel the desire of my thoughts when I am forces by the exuberant nature of my dreams to look through the filters of my mind. I see my life with him coming together and turn out to be a happiness ever after utopia. In the back of my mind, I believe Momma Mamie never is wrong about anything that she tells me. Within my soul, I believe that me and John are two people in love. I believe that the love that we share between each other will protect use from the hurt of any adversity that may arise for us."

In listening to the words of Momma Mamie, Rick believed in his heart that the adversity that she sees for their love cannot fight its way through the storm of it. Momma Mamie convinced him that the ways in which he wanted to live his life was wrong before God.

So Rick said unto Diamond, "So see, Diamond, I decided to let him go far from my heart because I am trapped inside this prison of a body. This body is the thing that is keeping me from the love of my life. So you see, I had to call him and tell him that I would be leaving and going coming back to Miami to take care of some business. It all happen because of Momma Mamie's fashion way of thinking. She has broken my dream into pieces of ever loving him. When he asked to see me before I left New Orleans, I told him that it would not be a good idea. I told him with all the strength that I had inside me. I said to him that we would no longer need to see each other ever again. At that moment, it just broke my heart into pieces. It was if the very soul within me was dying, gasping for its oxygen of love. From that point on, I didn't know what to do."

Rick began crying and sat down on the bed. Diamond got up from her seat in front of the mirror and walked over to bed where he was sitting and sat next to him. Diamond grabbed him inside his arms and said, "Baby, everything will be just fine...you wait and see. Just wait and see. Tell me something, is this man in love with you and you know that you love him?"

Rick said, "Yes."

"Then, girl, dry your eyes, baby, and go get your man 'cause you only have one life to live. You need to live every moment to the fullest. Because at the end of the day, all you will have is you and your man, and all the people that have something to say or how you need to live your life will be some where chilling at the end of the day with their man laid up somewhere not worrying about you and yours."

"It's not that easy, Diamond."

"Girlfriend, you have to follow your own heart when it comes to your happiness and no one else happiness because when the end comes, no one will be standing in front of God for you and that the gospel truth."

That night before Rick went to bed, he lay across the bed, looking at the phone, hoping within himself that John would call. At that moment, he thought about what Momma Mamie said about how wrong it is for him to love him. Tears began to fill the wells of his eyes, as he lay there, staring at the phone with the desire to call him. Momma Mamie's words strained him, and he fell asleep. One thing

Rick did not know was that John had his secretary do a little bit of investigation work on his whereabouts. John had her track Rick down to see where he was going; he had her call his Momma Mamie for information of his address, not letting her know the reasons why she needed Madam Colleen's information. Once he found out Rick's location, he immediately rushed out of the church building and caught the first flight out of New Orleans to find the love of his life. Once he arrived he arrived in Miami, he caught a taxi to Diamond's apartment and was standing there, knocking at the door with a handful of white tulips. Once Diamond heard the knock at the door, she came downstairs and asked who it is.

The voice on the other side of the door said, "My name is Reverend John Austin. I am here looking for Madam Colleen. Is she here?"

Diamond said, "Hold on a minute. I must put on some clothes." Diamond knew who he was. She ran upstairs to alert Rick that John was at the front door. From hearing these words, Rick could not believe his ears. The question that lied in the back of his mind at that moment was, *How is it that he found me?*

Rick jumped out of bed. "I must get myself together. Go and answer the door."

Diamond rushed to his room and put on a scarf on his head and brushed on some makeup to camouflage his manly image; he then rushed downstairs to answer the door and let Reverend John inside. To Diamond's surprise, he was a very handsome, well-dressed man standing at the door.

John then said unto him, "Excuse me, ma'am, I am looking for a lady by the name of Madam Colleen. Is she here?"

Diamond, amazed by John's handsome looks, replied, "Yes. Please come inside." Diamond then called upstairs to Rick, saying, "Madam Colleen, you have a guess here to see you."

Once Rick looked downstairs and saw John standing with a handful of flowers in one hand and his hat in another, in front of the door. Tears filled the wells of his eyes.

John said, "Madam Colleen, I need to talk to you, about an important matter."

Rick walked down the stairs and hugged him and began to cry even more.

John said, "I am here now, baby, I am here."

As John was holding him tightly in his arm, Rick said, "Something within me told me that you would come. I just did not know when."

"Nothing could keep me from you. My heart was lonely without you."

"My heart was lonely without you too."

Diamond stood in the background, crying his heart out, because he had never seen two people who could love each other so much.

Rick asked John to have a seat. "I am sorry you had to find me dressed in my night clothes."

John said, "That's okay. You look even more beautiful."

Rick then smiled. "Why, thank you. Give me a moment so I can get dress."

After Rick got dressed, they took a drive to the beach. As they walked along the side of the seashore, John began to tell Rick, "You know, Madam Colleen, during my time dwelling in this world, I have been many places, and I have seen many beautiful things, but I have never seen anything in this world as beautiful as you. It comes a time in a man's life when he desires the need to settle down. There is nothing more than I would like to do than get to know you better. You are the type of lady that a man dreams about being with. It is my hope that you would move back to New Orleans so that we can get to know each other better."

Rick said, "I don't know, John."

"Just think about it. I think I am falling in love with you. Every moment that I am away from you, every inch of my being is lonely without you."

After walking along the seashore, John kissed Rick on his cheek, and he headed back to New Orleans.

Chapter 20

That night when Diamond got in, Rick was sitting on the coach thinking on the conversation that he and John had, about him moving back to New Orleans to stay so they could get to know each other better and to allow their relationship to grow even more.

Diamond said unto Rick, "To tell me everything, girl, about what ya'll talked about! What did he say to you?"

Rick tried to be calm, but he could not hold his excitement. "Girl, it was the best day of my life. He really love me! It cannot be nothing but true love. For him to come this long way and find me, we are destine to be together forever. He has asked me to come back to New Orleans and stay so we can get to know each other better."

"Well, what are you going to do?"

"At this point, I come to the realization that once a person find love they should not ever let anything stand in the way of it. I believe that love only comes once in a lifetime, and I am not going to let it pass me by."

"While, girl, how are you going to keep the secret that you are a man from him?"

"At this point, I do not know what I am going to do, but there is one thing I am sure of—that I want to love, and it will give me the answer that I need to continue loving him for a lifetime."

"What are you going to do about your Aunt Mamie?"

"I love Momma Mamie. I know that she wants the best for me, but I have only one life to live, and I am going to live it for me. I know that my Momma Mamie loves me, and I can tell her about anything. I know she will understand why it is that I doing what it is that I am doing. She is the type of person that will let me make my on decision no matter how bad and sinful she might think it is."

Chapter 21

The next day, Rick called Momma Mamie and told her that he wanted to move back to New Orleans. Within a few days later, he did. Once he arrived, Momma Mamie was happy to see him, not knowing the reason why he decided to move back. That night over dinner, Momma Mamie said unto him, "So tell me, child, did you move back her to bother that man?

Rick said, "I am in love with him, Momma. He is the best thing I have ever happen to me. I know what you are going to say, just hear me out. Momma, I tried to take your advice and leave him alone and forget about him because it was the right thing to do. When I got to Miami, I was so very badly trying to paint the picture of our love out of my mind. Every time I erase the idea out of my mind, my heart re-sketched the idea of it back again. And that's when it happen. The next morning when I awaken, there he was, knocking on my door and stand on my front doorstep."

Momma Mamie said, "What are you say? He came down and found you, child?"

"You see, Momma, why we are destine to be together."

As tears fell from his eyes, Momma said, "If that's the case and you say that you are so in love with this man, why is it that you did not tell him the truth about you being a man and not woman?"

Rick turned and walked toward the window of the living room and looked out, speechless, thinking about why he did not tell John the truth. "Momma, have you ever been beat and rape by someone you thought was suppose to love you like that of a father? Who took that love inside your small heart and smash it down to there was no more left inside you?" As Rick turned and looked at Momma Mamie, he went on to say, "Momma, there was nights when I would wake up crying from nightmare, thinking within a matter of second he would come again and try to rob me of the manhood that my soul was hoping to have in the near future of my creation. When I awoke from those horrible nightmares, I would look around my room for the love of my mother, and she was not there to rock me back to sleep. I would get inside the closet of my room and hide and cry myself to sleep from fear, thinking to myself that I was alone. I would wake up cry sometimes, and Mother would ask me what was wrong. I could not tell her what it was actually that torments my soul. I feared what he might do to the both of us. I had no one to love me the way my soul said that it needed to be love. Momma, I have tried to love until I am blue in the face. Men have use my heart for money and gain. When I have tried to love in the past, it got me beaten to the point where I had to stay in the hospital for months at a time. Momma, since I saw Reverend John for the first time, and he smiled at me, he gave me light in the most darkest placcs of my life. He has caused me to believe without a shadow of doubt that he loves me for what lies inside of me rather than what lies on the outside of this body that God has curse me with.

"When he stood there at my front door, I could not tell him the truth for I did not want to break his heart like my heart has been broke for so many year by the ones that I thought loved me the way I love them. Momma, you make asked the question how I will pull this off. You know, Momma, I don't have the answer to that question now. But you know what, there is only one thing that I do know and that is, I am going to love him with all that I have to give, and love will help us climb the high peaks of difficulties that may arise and tried to hinder the love that we have between us both. Please, Momma, don't try to stop me for a life without him and you, I would rather take a knife and cut the very veins that are connected to my heart and died if I cannot have your love and his love next to me."

Momma Mamie said, "I see that no matter what I say, you have made up your mind. I just want you to know that I love you, son, and I'm going to leave this matters in the hands of God. All your life, I have taken you to church to show you right from wrong, child. Whatever decision you make and whatever makes you happy, you will always have the love of your old Momma Mamie by your side. It is my pray, child, that this desire that you have inside your heart will not destroy you. It my pray, baby honey child, that the good Lord up above will help you see your wrong and change your life before the good book of like is closed on you."

They then hugged each other and cried. At that moment, Momma Mamie accepted Rick's decision because her love for him covered the hills of his sins.

Chapter 22

Once Rick moved all his things to New Orleans with Momma Mamie, it was a whole new world for him. He was heavily involved in the church, worked even closer with the oil company, and he became the ladies' spokesperson for the organization of Momma Mamie. In the city of New Orleans that year, he raised more money for the underprivileged kids and orphans, who could not afford to go to college. He and John would spend a lot of time together, having dinner and late night walks in the park, holding each other as they explored the love of each other's hearts. When they would spend romantic afternoons at his house, sometimes the human flesh would try and take over John, but because of his declarations to God, he never let it cause him to touch or kiss Rick in a unpleasant way. This allowed Rick to keep his secret even more confined to his heart. One night while Rick and John were sitting under an old oak tree, they held each other's hand and talked about how beautiful life would be if they could spend it together forever.

That same night, John said unto Rick, still not knowing that he was a man, "Madam Colleen, I have been thinking long and hard about the times we have spent together. I want you to know that I have been having a wonderful time with you. I have never met a lady who could make me feel the way that you make me feel." Reverend John pulled out a ring. "Will you marry me?"

This was a surprise to Rick; it caught him off guard. With tears in his eyes, he said yes, without any thought of his state of being a man. He then kissed him on his lips for the first time. That kiss made Rick melt inside. Once John left him that night, Rick rushed up to his room with excitement in his heart. Once he laid a crossed the bed, reality kicked in. *My god, what have I just done?* At that moment, he did not know what he was going to do. One thing he did know was that he was not going to tell Momma Mamie about his excitement. He knew that her little heart would not be able to stand the news of the great sin that was about to happen. He then continued to lie inside his bed, hoping within his soul that love would give him an answer. He then decided to call Diamond to talk to her about his situation. "I needed to come back to Miami to talk to you about the problems that I am now facing concerning me and John. Girl, he has ask me for my hand in marriage, and I do not know what to do."

Diamond said, "What? He asked you to marry him?"

"I must go. I will tell you everything once I get there in the morning."

Diamond said, "Okay, hurry."

The next morning, Rick had breakfast with Momma Mamie. He told her that he would have to travel back to Mamie to take care of some important business.

Momma Mamie said with a suspicious look on her face, "Child, what are you up to now?"

"Nothing. I just have to go and take care of some important business. Before you worry, it will only take me a couple days, and I will be back."

Momma Mamie knew that there was something not right about the trip. She just looked at him in a strange way. "Okay, child, be safe and hurry up and come back."

Rick then called John and told him that he needed to meet with him.

John asked him, "Is everything all right?"

Rick said, "Everything is okay, baby. I just need to meet you tomorrow over lunch to discuss an important matters."

"Okay, let's say about twelve o'clock tomorrow afternoon."

"That will be great. I will meet you at our favorite restaurant."

The next day, Rick and John met for lunch. Once they were seated out on the back of the restaurant. Rick said unto John, "My, don't' you look handsome."

John said, "Thank you, Madam Colleen. So you say that you will be leaving, what's the hurry?"

"Oh, it's nothing very important. I'm going back to tell my best friend, Diamond, about our engagement, and so she and I can start making plans for the wedding."

"Forgive me for asking. I would think by this be a big event for you. I would think that you would allow Madam Mamie to help you with all of the arrangement."

"Why of course she will help me with the major parts of the wedding. The reason I want to travel back to Miami to talk to Diamond, I just want to personally tell her in person the existing knew and to get her involve, by it be she is my best friend and all. Don't worry, I will be back with in a few days."

"Would you like for me to drive you to the airport on tomorrow afternoon?"

"Yes, that would be great. My plane will be leaving at noon."

"I will be there to put you up, let's about eleven o'clock."

"That will be fine. I will be waiting."

Rick knew with in himself that he had to something, but he just did not know what. He figured Diamond would help him come up with something to do in helping him keep his secret, or he could tell John the truth in a way that he would not decide to leave him forever. The next morning, Reverend John arrived at Momma Mamie's doorstep and rang the doorbell to pick Rick up, to take him to the airport. When Reverend John rang the doorbell, Joe answered the door. To his surprise, it was John, standing there with his snow-white hat and suit on, with a cane on his hand.

John asked him, "Is Madam Colleen ready to go to the airport?"

Joe said, "Right this way," leading him into the living quarters.

"Who is it, butler?" Momma Mamie met them on their way there. To her surprise, it was Reverend John. "Well, hello, reverend, what brings you our way this morning?"

Reverend John as he took off his hat. "Why, I am here to see Madam Colleen off to the airport."

Momma Mamie said, "Oh really? Madam Colleen did not tell me that you would be taking her him to the airport."

"Madam Colleen may have forgot to alert you that I would be assisting here in this matter."

"I very sure she did. Well, son, Mr. Butler will show to the living quarters. While you are waiting, I will go and see if Madam Colleen is ready and let her know that you are here to pick her up for the airport."

Momma Mamie went upstairs to Rick's room and knocked on the door.

Rick said, "Who is it?"

Momma Mamie said, "It's your Momma Mamie, child."

"Come in."

When Momma Mamie entered the room, she found him sitting in front the mirror, bushing his hair. "Child, the reverend is downstairs waiting for you, to take you to the airport. Son, this is getting out of hand. You have this man coming to take you to the airport. I don't know what going through your mind is. I do not know what you are thinking. Don't you know sooner or later this man will find out who you really are? What, you think you can go on camouflage as a woman, leading this man to believe that you a woman when you know that you are a man? Child, don't you know that that man has needs. What are you going to do when he started to desire you in the interment sense? Baby honey child, you are just looking for trouble."

"There is nothing to worry about. Somehow, some way, I will find the answer to that question."

"You foolish child, are you crazy? There is no answer. You must stop this foolishness while you are still ahead. You are going to bring shame on this family and hurt to yourself. I have had enough, Rick. Do you hear me? I have had enough." She then turned and walked out of the room.

On her way downstairs, she stopped by the living quarters and said unto Reverend John, "Madam Colleen will be with you shortly."

Reverend John said, "Thank you, Madam Mamie." She then turned and walked to her room.

Once Rick was ready, he came downstairs and walked inside the living quarters, where Reverend John was sitting. Once he saw him walking inside the room, he stood and said, "Hello, Madam Colleen, my, don't you look beautiful on this fine morning of this Lord's day."

Rick said, "Why thank you, Reverend John, for your compliment. I am ready to go."

John grabbed Rick's bags before they walked out of the doors of the mansion. "Will you not allow Madam Mamie to see you off?"

"Momma Mamie is not feeling will this morning. She has already said her good-byes. We must hurry so I can catch the flight."

On they're way to the airport, Reverend John said unto Rick, "Madam Colleen, are you sure everything is okay?"

"Everything is okay. I just have a lot on my mind, nothing you need to worry your little soul about, my handsome man you." John smiled from hearing these words from Rick.

Once Rick arrived in Miami, he caught a taxi to Diamond's apartment. He walked up to Diamond's doorstep and just stood there with a great burden on his back, the burden of not knowing how he would keep his secret concealed from the love of his life. He then knocked on the door; Diamond opened it. Rick stood there with his bags with tears running down his face. Diamond said, "Oh, girl, what wrong now?" He then grabbed Rick and hugged him. "Baby, everything will be find. We will figure out something. Let me help you with your bags. Come in and sit down. Girl, you look a mess."

Rick said once he sat down, "Girl, I don't know what I am going to do. John has ask me to marry him. Momma Mamie told me before I left that I have lost my mind because sooner or later, he will find out about me."

"Have you told your aunt about the proposal?"

"Are you crazy? If I told her that, she would just have a heart attack and just die. The major problem is now I have told John that I would marry him before I really thought he it was that I am. Diamond, I am in love this is my chance at love, and I do not what to lose it. I must find away to keep this from him. He must not know. I do not know what I am going to do, Diamond, please help me find away that will help me keep him in my life. I can not lose him, please, me please." He then broke down, crying, saying, "Please help me, Diamond, I do not know what I am going to do."

"Stop crying, stop crying. Everything is going to be just fine. I have something to ask you."

Rick wiped the tears from his eyes. "Yes?"

"Tell me, girl, how much do you love him?"

"I love him so much I will give my life for him. I mean, I will do anything to keep him."

I have been doing some thinking since the last time I talked to you. What if I told you I have an answer to all your problem, and that you would not have to die to keep your mind? First, I must ask you how while do you like the life of living as a women?"

"I love the life of dressing like a woman. This is who I am."

"What if I told you that I know if a way in making you a woman permanent, and Reverend John will never know that you were ever a man."

"What? Is that possible? What do you mean? How can that be done, and I have the gifts that God has given me?"

"Once night when I was dance at the club, there was a man there. He asked me about transforming me in to woman, and I asked him what he meant about change me into a woman. He said he would change this thing between my legs into the gift that gave a woman."

"Are you sure? I have never heard of anything like this before done. I don't know, Diamond."

"He said he could do it. Before you came here, I looked inside my purse to find his number and called him to see if he could really do this, and he said yes. I do not know how it will turn out. At this point, girl, you really don't have too many chooses. It's this, or tell him the are do not ever see him again."

"I guess this is the only way, because I can not lose him, Diamond. This is my one chance at love, and I will not miss out on it. Momma Mamie will have to understand, somehow some way, I will find a way to tell her about this once it is done. Diamond, where is he located?"

"He is right in, Mamie. Rick, are you sure this is what you want to do? Girl, you need to seriously think about this really hard. Because once it is done, there is no turning back. Girl, I must tell you that there are no guarantees that there will be no side effects from the surgery."

"I am very sure I must do this. This is the only way."

"When do you what to me with the doctor to set up a date to get it done?

"As soon as possible. Is it possible that I can meet him on tomorrow?"

"I will call him right now to see if he can meet with us on tomorrow."

"Call him. I need do this right away."

Diamond walked over to the phone and looked inside the desk drawer and found the number; she began to dial the number. Once the doctor answered the phone, Diamond said, "Hello, Dr. Moore, my name is Diamond. I have a friend that is here visiting with me that needs to talk to you about your services. I want to know when can we come in and meet with you and talk to you about the surgery."

The doctor told Diamond that they must keep this matter very confidential, and that they can come in at one o'clock in the afternoon. Diamond hung up the phone and walked over to where Rick was sitting. "The doctor's name is Tommy Moore. He told me that we can come tomorrow at one o'clock." Diamond then hugged Rick. "Don't worry, everything will be okay, girl."

"Girl, I hope so. Do you understand why I have to do this? If I lose him, I will be all alone." When Rick spoke these words to Diamond, he began to cry on Diamond's shoulder.

That next afternoon, Diamond took Rick to visit the doctor who would change his life from that of a man into a woman. Once Diamond and Rick got into the building, they noticed that it looked like an abandoned warehouse or something. They walked inside, and there was a woman sitting at a desk, smoking a cigarette. Diamond said unto her, "We are here to see Dr. Moore. Are we in the right place?"

The woman said, "Yes, you are, waiting one minute." She got up from her chair and walked to the back. She then walked back to the front where Diamond and Rick was standing. At that moment, Rick was really nervous. She told them, "The doctor will see you now."

Once they entered the room, the doctor stood and said, "Hello, Diamond, what can I do for you today?"

Diamond said, "This is my friend, Rick. He want to talk to you about the surgery that can change him from a man to woman."

The doctor said unto Rick, "Hello, Rick, it is a pleasure to me you. Please have a seat. I must tell you that you first must be very sure this is something that you really want to do. Son, are you sure you are ready for this? Because once it is done, there is no turning back."

Rick said, "Yes, I am ready more than ever, but forgive me for asking, doctor. I have never heard of this be done ever in my life."

"This is true because you will be the first person ever in history to get such a thing like this done."

"How do you know that this surgery will work, and how do you know that it will not kill me?"

"Faith is a very power thing. When you believe in something, you will never fail. To answer you answer question, I do not know if it will work or even the fact that will kill you. It just depend on how strong you body is. You have a 50 percent chance of survival. Darling, the reason you must be very sure that this is something that you are will and ready to do. There is one good thing about, if you survey the surgery, you, my man, will make history. I will give you a couple of weeks to think about it. I will have the lawyer draw up the paper walk. Once you make up your mind, I want you to have Diamond give me a call, and we will begin the surgery, I will give you two weeks to think this thing through. Do you have any question?"

"How much will some things like this cost, and how long will it take for me to recover?"

"Five thousand dollars cash and about six month to recover."

"I will have Diamond call you in two week to let you know of my decision. Thank you, doctor. I will be getting back with you real soon."

Diamond and Rick got out of the chairs in which they were sitting and left the building. On their way back home, Rick said unto Diamond, "What do you think?"

Diamond said, "It's a tough decision to make. I like living, and no man will cause me to put my life on the line like that. But it your life, you have to ask yourself within, do you really love this man and can you live without him? It all up to you, either or I will be right beside you the whole way."

Rick turned and looked out the back window of the taxi with tears running down his face. That night when Rick was lying across the bed in a deep thought, Diamond knocked on the door and said, "Rick girl, are you sleep?"

Rick said, "No, come in."

Diamond walked inside the room. "What are doing?"

"Nothing, just laying here thinking."

Diamond sat on the bed and ran his fingers through Rick's long beautiful hair. "What are you thinking about, baby?"

"Just thinking about Reverend John and how much he makes me smile and how he makes me warm inside. You know, Diamond, there is nothing I would not do to keep his love, even if death so happen to take me on that operation table, it would be better for me rather than spend the rest of my life with out him apart of it."

Diamond just sat there and said nothing for at the back of his mind, he feared for his best friend's life, hearing the danger that the surgery may cause. Rick said unto Diamond, "I have been thinking, I think I will be leaving on tomorrow afternoon fly back to New Orleans to spend time with John before I get the surgery done."

"How are you going to explain to them about the long time you will be away from home?"

"I do not know what I will tell them, but I will come up with something."

The next afternoon, Rick headed back to New Orleans. While on the plane, he was in grave distress because of the decision he had to make about his life—to love or die being alone. He knew that if he changed the body that the good Lord above had given him, into that which is unnatural to that of a woman, he knew in his heart that he would bring a great burden upon himself, but the love of his life didn't leave any room for doubt. It was something he had to do for he never even knew such love existed. When Rick arrived in New Orleans, he caught a taxi back to his Momma Mamie's house. When he entered inside the house, he did not see anyone. He then proceeded upstairs quietly, trying not to awake his Aunt Mamie. Little did he know that she was not sleep. She was sitting inside the study, reading her Bible. She said unto him, "Ricky, is that you, son?"

Rick said, "Yes, Momma, it's me."

"My, I was not expecting you for another week or so."

"I just came back early to gather a few thing, and I will be heading out on tomorrow night."

"Why, child, what's on your mind?"

"Oh nothing, I just need to get away for while to get my thoughts together."

"Child, do you think I don't know you by now? What are you up to?"

"I am up to nothing. I'm just going away to get my life in order that's all, Momma."

"I hope that's all you are doing for God sakes."

"Momma, you have nothing to worry about. I think I will go to bed now."

"Child, have a good night's rest." As Rick turn to walk out the door, Momma Mamie said, "Remember, child, I love you regards of who you are, and I also what you to know that regardless of how hard I come down you, I only want the best for you, child, and I do not what anything to every happen to you. Rick, never be afraid to talk to me about anything. You hear me, child? I love you with all of my soul. I do not want you to feel that you are ever alone. Do you hear me, child?" Tears fell from both of their eyes.

Rick then walked over and hugged Momma Mamie and said, "Thank you, Momma. I love you too." After hugging and crying with Momma Mamie, he went up to his room and decided to call Reverend John. Once he answered the phone, Rick said, "Hello, darling, I know it's a little late. I decided to call you to let you know that I had made it back to New Orleans."

Reverend John woke up from his sleep. "Oh, that fine, Madam Colleen. I am happy to hear from. I was not expecting you to be back so soon."

"I had to come back to get a couple of thing. I will be leaving out again on tomorrow afternoon, heading back to Mamie."

"Why so soon? You just got back."

"I will tell you all about tomorrow over lunch."

"Okay, that will be fine. I will see you tomorrow. Have a good night's rest."

Rick said, "Okay, you do the same."

The next morning over breakfast, Momma asked Rick, "So, child, when will you be leaving for Mamie?"

Rick said, "This afternoon."

Would you like for me to get the car ready for you to go to the airport?"

"That would fine."

"Child, are you sure there is nothing that you do not have tell before you go?"

"Why no, Momma, why do you ask?"

"I don't know. Something in my spirit tells me that you are to something, and I can't put my finger on it. Child, I don't know what it is that you are up to. Be carefully because the curse of the madam is out to destroy you."

"Oh, Momma, I not worried about that old curse that your grandmother talked about. I will be just fine."

"Hush, foolish child, for you do not know what it is that you speak."

"Momma, you have nothing to worry about. I will be just fine."

"If there is nothing to worry about, tell me why I see weariness in your eyes, child."

"I am fine. I just need to get away to think for a minute. Mother, I have to go down to pick up something before I leave for out of town."

Momma Mamie said, "Okay, child, I want you to hear me and listen to me real good. I do not know what it is that you are up to. Whatever it is, you better forget about because it will destroy you for the rest of your life, or it may call death on your soul."

Rick then got from the table and went upstairs to get ready for his lunch date with Reverend John. Before he left the dining quarters, he said unto Momma Mamie, "Could you have the butler bring my car around to the front? I will be driving it today. I will see you later, Momma Mamie! I love you!"

"I love you too, baby honey child. Be careful."

Rick rushed out the door with excitement and got inside his red convertible Mercedes Benz and drove off. When he walked inside the restaurant, Reverend John was sitting, waiting on him. Once he saw Rick approaching the table where he was sitting, he immediately stood up to greet him. He then walked to Rick's side of the table and pulled his chair from underneath the table so he could be seated. Reverend John said unto Rick, "It is got to see you, my darling. Life has been lonely without you."

Rick grabbed his hand and said, "My fair man, I have been feeling the same way."

"So tell me, what's this, you tell me you will be leaving me again. What's the rush?"

"Well, the reason why I came back so soon and rushing back to Miami, me and Diamond have been talking about plan for me and your wedding. The reason why I came back was to get some clothing for the trip that we are taking to London, Paris, and France to shop for wedding dress and some more thing that we might need to make this wedding the best ever. I came back to talk to you about it to see you would be okay with it."

"Madam Colleen, you know that I will never stop you from anything that it is that you want to do. The that concern me is where will we get all this money from for you to go to all these places to shop for the wedding?"

"Need not to worry, I have enough money save to pay for these trips."

"How long do you expect to be gone?"

"For about four months. Need not to worry, I will call you every day while I gone."

"Is there anything thing I can do for you?"

"There is something you can do for me. While I am gone, I do not want you to breathe a word to anyone of our engagement."

"Madam Colleen, why?

"Because I want us to wait until I get back from my trip so the both of us will be together when we will announce it together. Okay, baby?"

"Okay, I will miss you while you are gone."

"And another reason why I really want this to be concealing between the both of us, I want to bake the news to Momma Mamie myself. I don't want it to get out before I tell her myself. I want you to know from this day and for the rest of our life, I will do everything in my power to keep the love between us a burning flame, if I have to die trying."

"I also want you to know every day from this day as long the good Lord above keeps my eyes open to look at your beautiful face, I shall protect your heart with the strength of my life."

Rick knew if the word got out before his makeover is done and he hasn't told Momma Mamie himself, she would have a heart attack. Once Rick get on the airplane, he had made up his mind that he would do the surgery even if it would risk his life. He knew that it was the only thing he could do in order to keep John a part of his life. Once he made it back to Miami, he told Diamond that he had decided to have the surgery done.

Diamond asked him, "Are you sure you're ready to take that big stand into ladyhood?"

Rick said, "Yes, I am ready. Sometimes a person will do anything for love."

"What did your Momma Mamie have to say about this?"

"She does not know. I knew if I told her, she would tried to stop me. I decided to do it on my own. After it's done, then I will tell her. Then we will have a wedding to attend, and you are going to be my matron of honor!"

"Me your bridesmaids," Diamond said, with excitement all over her face. "Girl, this is something that I have always dreamed of doing!"

"But, girls, you cannot let anyone know that you are a man."

"Girl, please, do I look like I have any manly characteristic about myself? I would be the best damn bridesmaid that has ever walked down the aisles of New Orleans. This is the greatest opportunity that a little old girl like me can ever have. I cannot wait to help you start planning to become the first lady of Mount Zion Baptist Church. Who knows maybe when I get there for this fine wedding of yours, I just might snatch me up one of these fine preachers like that one you got." The both of them laughed together. Soon after the conversation that Rick and Diamond had, they began to talk about the surgery.

The next morning, Rick had Diamond call the doctor to let him know that he had decided to have the surgery. The doctor made an appointment for Rick to come into his office in three days so that they could begin the surgery. Diamond and Rick arrived at the doctor's office about seven o'clock that Thursday morning. Before entering inside, Diamond said, "We are here. When you get this surgery, you will no longer be Rick Smith. You will transform in Madam Colleen." Rick was very nervous. Diamond saw the fear inside his eyes and said, "It's not too late. We can turn around right now and forget all about it."

Rick said, "No, this is something I must do."

"Are you sure?"

"Yes."

"Remember, I love you and will be right here with you the whole time. Everything will be just fine." Diamond opened the door and allowed Rick to walk inside first, and he then followed.

The doctor was standing inside the office, waiting for them. "Are you ready?"

Rick said, "Yes."

The doctor said, "Right this way."

Rick and Diamond followed him to the back to a little room with a bed and a table, with a white cover and sharp knives on it. The doctor said, "Diamond, I would like for you to sit in my office while I do the surgery."

Diamond said, "No, I want to go with him."

Rick said, "Diamond, it's okay. I will be fine."

Diamond asked the doctor, "How long will this take?"

"Four hours the most." Dr. Moore and Rick went inside the room and closed the door while Diamond waited inside the doctor's office. Once Rick and the doctor were alone, inside the room, Rick took off all his clothing and put on a gown. Then doctor reached inside a drawer and pulled out a needle with painkiller inside it. He told Rick, "Here is something for pain. It might not help much, but it is something." Once the doctor gave him the pain medication, he gave Rick a towel with a very strong odor on it that smelled like vinegar and told him to put this towel over his nose if the pain gets unbearable. The doctor then told Rick to open his legs before he began the surgery. He tied down Rick's arms and legs and told Rick before he began, "Cutting this will hurt a little a bit, so stay as still as you can." Once the doctor began cutting it, Rick screamed and screamed until the pain knocked him unconscious.

When Diamond heard the screaming, he rushed to the door of the room, beating on the door, saying, "You let him out of there. You let him out of there." He then fell to the floor on the outside of the room, crying, saying softly, "Please let him out of there."

Once the doctor finished operating, he checked his pulse to see if he was still alive. To his surprise, he found one! He then said unto him, "My lady, you are finish."

Rick at this point had changed himself from Rick to Madam Colleen. Once it was over, Dr. Moore put Rick, who was still unconscious at the time, in another room. Once she woke up from the surgery, Diamond said unto her, "You are now officially Madam Colleen."

Because of Rick's drowsiness, he said to Diamond, "There is something wrong with my body."

"You are just getting adjusted to the surgery, just get you some rest."

Madam Colleen fell back to sleep. As he began to heal while she was in the recovery room, he called John to let him know that she was doing fine, and that he would have a fine wedding dress.

John understood, he said, "Okay, take your time."

Within the two days of having the surgery, he caught a bad fever and infection to the point it almost killed him. Diamond was right by him side for support. Three weeks later, the fever and infection dropped and began to heal. On the seventh week, he had gained just enough strength for Diamond to take him home. The doctor would come over to Diamond's house to check on him, to make sure everything was well with him. Once he got to feeling well enough, he decided to call Reverend John, to let him know that he was all right. Rick called Reverend John; he was at the church. He answered the phone and said, "Hello, Mount Zion Baptist Church."

Madam Colleen said, "Hello it me, Colleen."

"Where have you been? I have been worrying about you. I have heard from you in about a month. Is everything all right?"

"Everything is fine. For the past few weeks, I had a very bad fever, and it made me really sick."

"What, a fever? Why didn't you call me and let me knows? Are you okay?"

"I feel great. Need not worry, I am just fine."

"Where are you? I will come where you are to see you."

"I am in France. There is no need for you to come here. Besides I will be home in couple of weeks."

"Madam, I do not understand why it is you did not call me and let me know that you were sick?"

"The reason I did not call was I did not want you to worry yourself. It was just a little fever, nothing more."

"I miss you so much. How is the shopping going?"

"I miss you too. For as the shopping, I have went everywhere, and I still have not found the right wedding dress. When I come home, I think I will let Momma Mamie help me."

"I have to go I have a meeting to attend. Hurry back home. I love you."

"I love you too, and John, I promise I will never stay way from you long like this ever again."

"Okay, my love, I have to go." And the then hung up the phone.

Later, Momma Mamie begin the worry because Rick had not called her in weeks, not knowing what it is was that he had done to his body. Momma Mamie decided to call him one night. "Child, a bad spirit has come over my soul telling me that, baby honey child, you have done something that you have no business doing."

Rick said unto her, "Momma, you have nothing to worry about. I am better than I have ever been in my life. Momma, I am going to tell you all about it when I get back to New Orleans in a couple weeks."

Little did Madam Colleen know, his problem was just the beginning. Momma Mamie said, "Okay, child, you know Momma Mamie knows. You cannot pull the wool over my eyes."

Rick hurried her off the phone. "Okay, Momma, I will talk to you when I get back home. I have to go."

"Okay, child." And then Momma Mamie hung up the phone.

Once Madam Colleen felt he was well enough, he decided to call John to let him know that he would be coming home on Saturday afternoon, three weeks from the last time he talked to him. John asked her did he have any luck in finding a dress, he then said, "There were so many to choose from. I could not make up my mind, so I am going to get you to help me make the final decision in picking it out." Inside Madam Colleen's heart, he knew he had not looked for any dresses. John told him to hurry back home for he could not wait to see her. John was so happy to hear that he was coming home, still not knowing her secret.

Chapter 23

When she arrived at the airport on that Saturday afternoon, Reverend John was standing there with the world biggest smile on his face, with a handful of flowers in is hand. Once Rick walked unto him, he kissed him on the cheek and said unto him, "I have longed to see you, my handsome man."

John picked him up in his arms, bursting with excitement. They decided to go out for dinner and spend time together. While they were eating, John looked across the table and said, "Baby, there is something different about you."

Madam Colleen said, "Do I look bad?"

"Oh no, it just something that is different. I guess I just have seen you in a while."

Before Madam Colleen came back to New Orleans, the doctor had given him some pills that would grow his breast. Maybe the tissue he was using to make it appear like he had breast was sitting on his rising chest. At that moment, he became nervous. As he was rubbing John's hand, he said, "Yes, maybe it's because you have not seen me in a long time, honey that's all.

"Maybe that's the case. Never mind that. Tell me all about your trip."

"I had a wonderful time being away. The trip also help me to see how to love you even more."

"Great, baby. You know ever since you left, I have been missing you to the point some nights worrying if you were all right."

"I have been missing you too, with all my heart."

"Now that you are back, is it all right if I tell my mother of my engagement to the love of my life?"

"Yes, you can tell anyone you like because I am here to stay and love you until the end of time." At that moment, he knew that he was officially Madam Colleen in her full attire. He also knew that he was the next madam who would supersede the legacy of Momma Bea.

After dinner, John drove Rick to Momma Mamie's house and dropped her off. Momma Mamie was there, waiting in her study, reading the good book of God's word. When Rick got inside the house, he walked inside the room where she was sitting and said, "Momma, I am home!"

She stood and opened her arms. "Child, it's good to have you back."

"Thank you, Momma."

"Come here, child, and give me a hug."

Once they hugged each other, Rick said, "Momma, I have something to tell you."

Momma Mamie took her seat and looked him in his eyes. "What is it, child? What have you done, child?"

Rick then raised his left hand and showed the engagement ring that Reverend John had given him. "Look, Momma, Reverend John done ask me for my hand in marriage."

When Momma Mamie heard these words, her heart dropped to the floor, speechless. After she got over the shock that hit her soul, she said, "Child, have you gone crazy? Have you forgotten that you are a man? Rick, do not do this to me. I am tide of you and this foolishness. Lord, ham mercy. Lord, ham mercy. Child, how are you going to marry this man in the state that you are in? Don't you know sooner or later, he is going to find out who are you. That man will kill you die if he find he has married a man, and it would serve you right. Rick, you cannot go around playing with folk's hearts. You will get seriously hurt. Do you hear me?"

"That will never happen, Momma, He will never find out that I was ever a man."

"What do you mean he will never find out?"

Rick spread his arms. "Momma Mamie, I have brought you the madam that will supersede the legacy of Momma Bea."

"What are you talking about, foolish child?" She stood up out of her chair and started walking toward Rick. Slowly, tears began to fall from his eyes as the words of his unrevealed truth began to climb upon his tongue. Momma Mamie said, once she got close to him, "Child, what have you done?"

"Momma, while I was away in Miami, I had a sex change."

"What do you mean, child?"

"I have changed myself from a man to a woman...see... my breast are real breast. They are growing every day."

Momma Mamie was shocked. Rick then grabbed her hands and placed it on his breast. Momma Mamie said, "My god child, what have you done."

"I have changed it down there too, Momma." He pointed to the missing gift God had given him. Momma Mamie looked down between his legs; she then moved her hand slowly down his body, from his breast until she placed it under his dress between his legs. Once she touched between his legs under his dress and realized that the gift of God was not there, she fainted. Just in the nick of time, Rick caught her before she hit the floor. Rick then called for Joe to help him carry her to the bed. Once Joe came into the room, he became nervous. "What has happened to Madam Mamie?"

Rick said, "She has pasted out from some shocking news that I have told her. She will be fine, just help me carry to her room."

The next morning when she woke up, she was just fine, sitting on the back deck, looking over her beautiful flower garden. Rick walked outside and saw her sitting. He walked over to where she was sitting and sat next to her, looking over the beautiful flower garden with her.

Momma Mamie the said, "You know, child, I have been praying to the good Lord above about this thing you have done to yourself. You know, baby honey child, in all my life, I have never heard of anything like this ever being done before. The world is changing day by day. Man is becoming wicker by the moment God is not please with the ways of man. I want you to know that I don't care what you do to your body. That's between you and God. It's your life and your decision. In spite of this great sin you have done to yourself, I want you to know that I love the spirit that lies inside your soul, child. You may change your body around to be something that God has not created you to be. But there is one thing you cannot change, inwardly, you will always be a man in the eyesight of God. You can go right ahead and marry that man. I not going to say a word, nor will I try and stop you. But there is one thing that I always want you to remember, when death look you in the eye because of this grave sin you have done, remember I told you so. It's is my prayer, child, that my curse of the madam will not bring blood to your head. I am afraid for you, child."

"There is nothing to be afraid about. Nothing is going to happen to me."

"For your sake, I hope so, because you are my child. I love in spite of your sin. Like I said a moment ago, if you want to go on and marry that man, I'm not going to try and stop you, child, because it is your life, but there is one thing that I want you to know, child, is that God is not please. I do not know what God has in store for your life. Baby, the ground that you are treading on is dangerous ground. Child, you know right from wrong. I not going to stop I can not stop you this some you and God got to take care," said Momma Mamie.

Momma Mamie quoted what Paul said in the Bible in Romans 1:16–28 (KJV):

> For I am not ashamed of the gospel of Christ: for it is the power of God unto salvation to every one that believeth; to the Jew first and also to the Greek. For therein is the righteousness of God revealed from faith to faith: as it is written, the just shall live by faith. For the wrath of God is revealed from heaven against all unrighteousness of men, who hold the truth in unrighteousness; Because that which may be known of God is manifest in them; for God hath showed if unto them. For the invisible things of him from the creation of the world are clearly seen, being understood by the things that are made,

even his eternal power and God head; so that they are without excuse. Because that, when they knew God, they glorified him not as God, neither were thankful; but became vain in their imaginations, and their foolish heart was darkened. Professing themselves to be wise, they became fools, And changed the glory of the incorruptible God into an image made like to corruptible man, and to birds, and four footed beasts and creeping things. Wherefore God also gave them up to uncleanness through the lusts of their own hearts to dishonor their own bodies between themselves: Who changed the truth of God into a lie, and worshiped and served the Creator, who is blessed for ever. Amen For this cause God gave them up into vile affections: for even their women did change the natural use into that which is against nature: And like wise also the men, leaving the natural use of the women, burned in their lust one toward another; men with men working that which is unseemly, and receiving in themselves that repentance of their error which was meet. And even as they did not like to retain God in their knowledge, God gave them over to a reprobate mind, to do those things which are not convenient.

"And that's the book, child. Now you take that and thank about what I have said unto you. I also want you to know that you are my child, and whatever decision you make, I cannot turn away from you." Momma Mamie then turned and hugged him, her eyes filled with tears. Momma Mamie then looked up to the heavens and said, "Momma Bea, baby honey child, I hope that you didn't turn over in your grave."

"I must tell you something."

"What is it, child?"

"On tomorrow, Reverend John and I will be announcing our engagement to the church on Sunday."

"Well, child, if this is what you want to do. You have made up your mind. This is between you and God. I must warn you, if you marry this man with this deceit inside your heart, the curse of the madam will fall upon your head, and there will be nothing that I can do about." She then got up from her chair and walked inside the house.

That Sunday morning before Reverend John preached his sermon, he said, "You know, church, I am happy this morning. The Lord has finally given me the gift I have been looking for my whole life. You know the Bible says, 'When you find a good woman, you find a good thing.'"

When he spoke these words to the church, Momma Mamie dropped her head in shame; she could not say anything but go along because of her fear of the shame that would come up on the church and the family—she decided that she would leave it in the hands of God.

The church then said, "Amen."

Reverend John said, "Have finally found the women of my dreams." He then called Madam Colleen up to the pulpit and continued, "I present to you Madam Colleen of whom I have asked for her hand in marriage."

At this point, the church gave a stand ovation as if she was the queen of the Nile, but Momma Mamie remained seated, with her head tilted, burdened by the great sin of her Rick. When she looked into Rick's eyes, she became happy because she has never seen her him happy as he was before. It was also a great burden on her little soul because she knew that Rick had been misused and abused his life. At this point, Rick had gone too far with his desire, and there was nothing she could do to stop it.

Chapter 24

The next couple of weeks, Momma Mamie gave Rick and John a wedding party on the back lawn of her house. It was decorated, so beautiful white flowers were everywhere with white chairs lined on the lawn. All the church members were there, along with her friends from the community—white and black. It was the most beautiful event a woman could dream of. After the party, Momma Mamie and Rick started planning the wedding that would go down in the history on the city of New Orleans.

During that time, Rick invited Diamond to come down to help. When Diamond walked of the plane, she was truly a lady a man will die for. That week was the best week of Rick's life; they went out to shop for the right dresses and the best wedding planners New Orleans had to offer. Rick didn't have any girlfriends he could invite as his bridesmaids, so he asked some of the sisters of the church to be in his wedding. John also flew in his mother, Mrs. Helen, who was the sweetest woman you'll ever meet. While they were out shopping for dresses, to wear to the wedding, by it being that the theme was that everybody had to wear hats. Rick and Momma Mamie convinced Mrs. Helen that she would look great in one, so she bought a hat and dress to match.

That night before the wedding, Rick was sitting in front the mirror, bushing his hair. While looking in the mirror, he noticed a strange old woman standing behind him who was dressed in an old, ragged hat and dress, who looked like a slave of many years ago.

"My, don't you have beautiful hair like yo' Momma Bulla," she said unto him, with a smile on her face. She then went on to say, "The old saying is true. That the apple does not fall to for from the tree." She then laughed.

Rick held the brush in his hand tightly, with fear running down the flesh of his body. He tried to turn around, to look face to face with the Zulu witch slave but was unable to do so because the force of her spirit would not allow him to do so.

The Zulu witch slave said unto him, "So tell me something, foolish child, when a man looks into a mirror and sees not himself, shall he call himself the mirror or the man." She then laughed out loud again. Rick could not respond because of the fear that rushed through his veins. The Zulu witch slave continued to say, "Your heart has been hardened with deceit and the lust of your flesh just like Bulla. I warned her, and she would not listen unto me that day in the field because of her desires of the flesh. Because of this, she cause the knife of the plantation owner's wife to fall on her throat, causing the life that God gives to be robbed from her soul. This night, you have the same desire in your heart that causes you to deceive this man into believing that you are something that you are not. If you quote those ancient marriage vows unto him on tomorrow and not harken unto the words in which I speak unto you on this night, I will cause a curse to fall upon your head that will cause your womb to bleed like that of a sheep that has gone to the slaughter. From the day you kiss him on the lips of truth with the deceitful lips of Judas, every year from the day you kiss him, the curse of the madam will haunt you to remind you of this great sin that you have done."

"Who are you? Are you the devil's child?"

The Zulu witch slave began to laugh and said, "I am surprise, child, that Mamie has not told you who it is that I am. I am the weary soul that has lasted for over a hundred years or more. I am the soul of a slave that was killed along with my white slave child, by a white man who deceived my heart into believing that he was in love with me and he wasn't. This man was the great-grandfather of the man that Bulla was in love with that lead her to her death."

"What is your name?"

"You foolish child, my name is Legend Mabel." After saying this, she disappeared.

That same night, while Momma was sleeping in her room, the Zulu witch slave walked through the walls of Momma Mamie's room and stood at the foot of her bed and said, "My Mamie, you have done well for yourself."

Momma Mamie heard her voice. "What is your business, demon?"

The Zulu witch slave began to laugh. "Now, Mamie, I have neither a problem nor business with you. It's Rick I have business with."

"You leave him be. Do you hear me? You leave him be."

"My, I have not seen you in over thirty year. Is this any to treat a guest? What would Bea say if she heard you speak these things to me? It is a shame that Ernestine could not live to see how well you are living in this house."

"I dare you speak of my grandmother's and my sister name. Speak your business and leave."

"My business is this, I have warned that boy of your that if he go and get married tomorrow that a curse will fall on his head like that of Bulla and Ernestine. If he is stubborn like them, he will share their same faith."

Momma Mamie said in a loud voice, "Get out of my house before I whip you to and fro around this room with God's word."

The Zulu witch slave disappeared quickly. Momma Mamie got out of bed and rushed down to Rick's room. She found him laying on the bed, crying in fear of the visit by the Zulu witch slave. Momma Mamie rushed over to him. "Son, are you okay?"

Rick said, "Momma, I am afraid."

"Child, you must stop this right now before that demon destroy your life or even kill you."

"I can't stop it now. All my life, I have dream of having someone who could really love me for me."

"Child, do he really love you for who it is that you are?"

"I know what you are trying to say. I know who it is that God has created me to be, and that is a man and Reverend John does not know that. But he does know me inwardly— the nice and kind person that lies behind this mask if a body that I am trapped inside of. Momma, I do not care what this demon is trying to do to me. She may come and trying to scare me, she may even take my life from me, but she can't and will not change the way I feel for him because you see, Momma, this that I feel inside is deeper than any river or ocean. One may trying to drain my ocean dry, but they cannot do it. I will not let them do it. You see, Momma, me and John's ocean are two in one and it run real deep. There is no stopping this love that I have inside my heart for him, so, Momma, you can just tell that oh slave of a demon who hunters and tries to destroy the black madam that she can do whatever she want. I would rather have my life be take from this world than to live inside this container of a body without his love beside. If death is the only thing that will stop me from being with him, let it take hold of me then, Momma, the hurt and this lonely heart of mine will be a rest from the challenges that fall upon me. And I will never have the chance to break John's heart. But if love allows me to live, I will love him with all my heart and soul. Momma, listen to me. You and John are all I have left in this world that really love me. Please, Momma, let me live my life, and maybe one day, if there is true a God like you saying, it is just maybe he will make a way for me to change my life back to what I was. Momma, do you really trust in this God the way you say you do?

"Yes, child, I do." Tears were falling from her eyes.

"Well, if he is real like you say he is, nothing, I mean nothing can destroy anything that you love, not even that demon slave." They hugged and went to bed.

Chapter 25

The day of the wedding, Reverend John's best friend D. M. Williams flew in to perform the wedding ceremony. All of John's preacher friends were also there; some were even groom's men. They all flew in from all over the world. The wedding was the most beautiful wedding a black girl could have ever dreamed of; white and pink tulips were everywhere. Everyone was there. Some of Mamie's white business associates were there with their wives. Many people were there from the community; there were a lot of the ladies from the ladies club. The wedding was held in Momma Mamie's back lawn.

Diamond walked down the aisle as if she was getting married herself. As Rick walked down the aisle, they had a lady singing at that wedding, who sounded like that of an angel. John was standing there with his white tuxedo on, smiling as if he had died and gone to heaven. Joe escorted him down the aisle that day. As Rick approached, John slowly took off his hat, as tears filled the wells of his eyes, with a slight smile and held it by his side. As Rick got closer, walking toward him, it was as if he was walking out the history of the adversity that tremble his own soul from his birth. This walk of happiness was not only for him; this walk was for Momma Bulla, Momma Bea, and Momma Chaney, Momma Georgia, Momma Ernestine, Momma Mamie, and his mother. Above all, it was to fulfill the legacy of Momma Bea and to fulfill his place as the seed of the madam. Little did he know that his curse was just the beginning. As he walked closer to the man of his dreams, he began to notice a sharp pain in the wound created that made him into a woman. He did not let it stop him from walking to the love his life. Once he made it to John and the preacher, they used an old quote from the old Asian philosopher who was well-known for humility. The preacher said unto them, "This a beautiful day in the Lord for these two youth people to get married at this time. We will allow the both of them to quote their vows unto one another." They then turned their backs to him and took their first step and said their vows unto each other.

John said, "My beloved, our love has become firm by your walking one step with me. Together we will share the responsibilities of the home, food, and finances. May God bless us with noble children to share. May they live long."

Colleen said, "This is my commitment to you, my lord. Together we will share the responsibility of the home, food, and finances. I promise that I shall discharge all of my share of the responsibilities for the welfare of the family and the children."

"Oh, my beloved, now you have walked with me the second step, may God bless you. I will love you and you alone as my wife. I will fill your heart with strength and courage: this is my commitment and my pledge to you. May God protect the household and children."

"My lord, at all times, I shall fill your heart with courage and strength. In your happiness, I shall rejoice. May God bless you and our household."

"Oh, my beloved, now since you have walked three steps with me, our wealth and prosperity will grow. May God bless us. May we educate our children, and may they live long."

"My lord, I love you with single-minded devotion as my husband. I will treat all other men as my brothers. My devotion to you is pure, and you are my joy. This is my commitment and pledge to you."

"Oh, my beloved, it is a great blessing that you have now walked four steps with me. May God bless you. You have brought auspiciousness and sacredness in my life."

"Oh, my lord, in all acts of righteousness (Dharma), in material prosperity (Artha), in every form of enjoyment, and in those divine acts such as fire sacrifice, worship, and charity, I promise you that I shall participate, and I will always be with you."

"Oh, my beloved, now you have walked five steps with me. May Mahalakshmi make us prosperous. May God bless us."

"Oh, my lord, I will share both in your joys and sorrows. Your love will make me very happy."

"Oh, my beloved goddess, by walking six steps with me, you have filled my heart with happiness. May I fill your heart with great joy and peace, time and time again. God bless you."

"My lord, may God bless you. May I fill your heart with great joy and peace. I promise that I will always be with you."

"Oh, my beloved, as you the seven steps with me, our love and friendship have become inseparable and firm. We have experienced spiritual union in God. Now you have become completely mine. I offer my total self to you. May our marriage last forever."

"My lord, by the law of God and the holy scriptures, I have become your spouse. Whatever promises I gave you, I have spoken them with a pure heart. All the angels are witnesses to this fact. I shall never deceive you, nor will I let you down. Forever I shall love you."

After quoting their vows, they then turned and walked back up to the preacher. He then said unto them, "The words in which you have spoken unto each other have conform your Holy commitment before God. If there is anyone that opposes this marriage, speak now or forever hold your peace." Momma Mamie hung her head in shame and allowed fear to take hold of her tongue. The preacher went on to say, "If there is not anyone that opposes this marriage, by the Holy Communion in God, I now pronounce you man and wife. You may kiss the bride!" Diamond busted out in tears because she was so happy for her friend; she had never seen anything so beautifully done before. Momma Mamie shed a few tears because she saw the happiness in Rick's eyes, regardless of what he was doing. They were then pronounced man and wife—Mr. and Mrs. John Smith. Rick's thirst for love has been finally quenched forever.

At the reception, everyone met and greeted the happily wedded couple. Momma Mamie convinced the both of them that after the wedding, they needed to stay at the mansion. She wanted the madam of the black seed to follow the history of the black madam by staying in the house of Momma Bea. Rick and John agreed to stay.

Chapter 26

That next morning after the wedding, when Rick awoke, he went inside the restroom. He noticed that he was bleeding really bad, and that he was not felling well. He became afraid because he did not know what was going on with his body. At that moment, the Zulu witch slave appeared and began laughing, saying, "You foolish child!" She then went away.

Rick then rushed down to the room where Diamond was sleeping. "I am bleeding really bad. I have sharp pain inside my belly. Diamond, I am afraid."

Diamond said, "Girl, we need to get you to a doctor!"

Rick then went upstairs into the bedroom where he and John were sleeping. John said, "Madam Colleen, what are you doing? Come back to bed."

Rick said, "Honey, I am not feeling well. I am bleeding."

John shouted, "You are bleeding!" He then said, "Do you want me take you to the hospital?"

Rick said as he was getting dressed, "No, baby, I will be just fine. This is something that ladies just go through from time to time. Beside, I have asked Diamond to go with me to the doctor to get me checked out."

"Are you sure? Have you told your Aunt Mamie?

"No, I have not told her because I do not want her to worry herself about me. It's really nothing."

"Call me and let me know something. I will be at the office at the church. Call me if you need anything." Rick gave him a kiss on the lips and walked out the door to head for the hospital.

As Rick was riding inside the car, he and Diamond noticed that the bleeding was getting worse to the point that it had turned the lower part of his dress red, full of blood. Rick was in much pain; he began to fear for his life. He said unto Diamond, with sweat and fever, "I believe I am dying. Call Momma Mamie and tell her what is going on with me. Do not call John. Please, Diamond, don't let him find out about my secret." He then passed out in the backseat of the car. Rick knew that the bleeding was from the surgery that transformed him from a man into a woman.

Diamond screamed out to the driver, "Hurry, she has passed out!" Diamond said unto Rick, "Girl, please do not die on me. You have some much to live for."

Once they arrived at the hospital, Diamond just out of the car and began to scream, "Someone please help us! Some please help. My friend is dying."

One of the nurses rushed out to get him. At that time, he had went in to a coma. Once the doctors took him in the back, Diamond called Momma Mamie and said, "Please hurry to the hospital. Rick is bleeding and has passed out."

Momma Mamie said, "Lord, ham mercy. I will be right there." Once she made it to the hospital, Diamond was hysterical. Momma Mamie said, "Calm down, child, tell me what happen."

Diamond said, "This morning, he awake me and said that he was bleeding, and that he was feeling pain inside his stomach."

"Hush, child, someone will hear you."

"I think that the bleeding is a resort of the surgery that he had in making him in to a woman. Something has went wrong with it."

"Do Reverend John know?"

"All he knows that he came to the doctor, but he does not know that he was doing this bad."

Momma Mamie said, "Good." She then called her private doctor to come and take of Rick. Once the doctor got there, Momma Mamie said unto him, "Whatever you find out about my child, you tell no one, not even her husband. You kept this between you and me and conceal all records. Do you her me, son?"

The doctor said, "Whatever you say." When he went in to see him and examined him, he noticed that his womb looked like a butcher had cut him up pretty bad. The insides of his womb had become infected; he had never seen anything like this before in his life. He soon found out that Madam Colleen was really a man rather than a woman while he was looking at the X-rays of her body. The doctor ordered emergency blood because she had lost a lot of blood. The reason Momma Mamie decided to keep this a secret from John is that she knew that if this secret got out, it would destroy a lot of people, including the church. Once the examination was over and the doctor gave Rick extra blood, it had begun strengthening him. The doctor said unto Momma Mamie, "Can I speak to you a moment."

Momma said, "Yes."

"I sorry to tell you from the examination that I done on your daughter. There is nothing else I cannot do for her. Not only that I have some more shocking news for you, I do not know how to tell you this, but your niece has a serious problem. The bleeding is happening from the resort of a surgery she had some time ago. Your niece is not really a woman but a man. He has had his penis cut off. In all the time that I have been a doctor, I have never seen a surgery perform like this before in my life. She needs to go back to the doctor that done this hideous thing unto her to see if he can fix it. If he does not get it fix, the next time it happen unto him, it just might kill him."

Momma Mamie said, "Oh my god! May I see her?"

"Yes, you can, but be very quiet because we do not what to disturbed her because the slightest disturbs could cause the bleeding to start again."

"Remember to tell no one of this."

"My lips are sealed."

Momma Mamie also said, "Tell the nurse to call her husband and let him know of his wife illness."

Once the nurse called the church office where Reverenced John was, his secretary walked inside his office and said, "I have just received word from the hospital that you need to hurry down to the hospital because Madam Colleen is not doing well."

John hurried and got his bag and drove down to the hospital to see how his wife was doing. He rushed up to the nurse's desk. "I am here to see my wife, Colleen Smith. How is she doing?"

Diamond walked up to the desk where he was standing. "Hi, John, the doctor said that she will be okay."

John asked, "Where is she?" At that moment, the nurse had went and got the doctor. John asked the doctor, "How is my wife?"

The doctor said, "She will be just fine. She has a very bad bleeding between his legs. We have stop the bleeding for now, and we have gave her extra blood so she should be just fine for now."

John then asked, "What is causing the bleeding?"

"As of this point, I have not found out what the problem is, but I will be working closely with her until the problem is found. Once she get to feeling better and she it released to go back home, I want you to pay very close attention to her. If you notice any blood or pain in her lower parts, I want you to contact me immediately."

"Okay, I thank you very much for your help. Where is she? Can I see my wife?"

"Yes, you can. She is sleeping from the pain medication that I gave her."

Once John and Diamond walked into the room, they found Rick sleeping, and Momma Mamie was sitting right beside him. John walked up to where Momma Mamie was sitting and said unto her, "How is she doing?"

Momma Mamie said, "She is doing well to be expected. She has been sleeping since I have been in here with her."

John looked at his lovely wife, and tears began to fall. His heart hurt from the thought that his wife was almost taken from him. Momma Mamie had become very tired and weary from the thought of losing her niece and the thought of keeping his secret. She said unto John and Diamond, "Children, I must go. I have became very tired. Ya'll take care of my baby. She is all I got left." She then got up out of her chair and walked slowly out of the room.

Two weeks later, Rick was released from the hospital. He was feeling great. A couple days later his release from the hospital, one morning when he awoke, he walked downstairs to find that Momma Mamie was not inside. She was outside, on the back desk, eating breakfast. He decided to walk outside, on the back deck. When she noticed that he was out there with her, she said, "Child, how are you feeling on this fine day that the Lord has made?"

Rick said, "Momma, I am feeling a whole lot better."

"That good, child." And Momma Mamie became silent.

"Momma, I want thank you for what you done for me. I know this is a lot on you right now. I wish it did not happen like this, but, Momma, I am in love."

"Child, I know what it is that your heart desire. This thing that you have done to yourself and the church, child, has cause the curse of the madam to fall down on your wound where it will cause you to bleed, and it just might kill you. Child, you better be very careful because that demon is out to take your life."

"Momma, who is she?"

"In time, you will find out all that you need to know about her for in time she will revile who it is that she is unto you. Child, I want you to know that I love you with all my heart and soul. Baby, the thing that makes my soul tremble is that if you do not let this man know who you really are and call off this marriage, the curse of your wound will kill you."

"Momma, I cannot do that because I just know that that the love that I have inside my heart and the love John has in his heart for me will not let the curse of the madam kill me. And you know what, Momma, if the curse by chase kill me, there is one thing I do know that when it laid my head to sleep, I will die knowing that someone finally loves me for what was inside me and not for my outward appearance and the thing that I have." Rick then got up out his seat and walked inside the house with a broken heart and tears inside her eyes. Momma Mamie just sat there in deep meditation, believing within her soul that the curse of the madam will take away another person whom she holds near to her heart.

From that point on, John and Rick traveled all over for his preaching engagements. John was an eloquent speaker; some people said that he had a voice like that of John the Baptist. Everyone loved to hear him speak. Rick was an extraordinary woman. When he walked inside the room with tailored made dresses and hats, the ladies at the conferences were amazed at his beauty and style.

During their travel across the country, Rick gained a lot of respect from the black women inside the church, even to the point where they would have him speaking at Lady Day's engagements. He did such a great job in speaking that they made him the president of the National Christian Women's Association. He was the voice of the ladies of the church. Soon after, he became the president of Momma Mamie's Elite Women's Club. During that same year, serving as the president of the Elite Women's Club, he raised over a hundred thousand dollars for several organizations, including orphans from the city of New Orleans. When Rick and John got back from his gospel meetings in Atlanta, Georgia, he told Rick that night in the bedroom, before he was getting in bed, while he was brushing his hair, "Madam Colleen, you know I've been thinking seriously about running for the mayor for the city of New Orleans in the upcoming election."

Rick then stood to his feet with a burst of excitement rushing through his veins. "Baby, that is a wonderful idea. I just know you will win with the help of Momma Mamie and me."

The next morning while they were eating breakfast in the dining quarters, Rick told Momma Mamie of John's desire in running for the next mayor of New Orleans.

Momma Mamie said, "Son, that's a wonderful thing."

Rick asked her if she could talk to some of her friends to let them know John's desire to run for the office of mayor and to see if she had a friend who can help him out with his campaign.

"I would love to," Momma Mamie said, with excitement bursting in her veins. "I never thought I would ever see the day when a man of this family would be running for the seat of mayor. Child, I just know with the help of you old Momma Mamie, I just might see about getting you that office. Now, son, tell me something. What is it that you want to do for this fine city in which we live in?"

John said, "I want to create new jobs for all black men and women and bring the unity gap between black and white people together, also making a way far more of our black humanitarians go to college."

Momma Mamie said, "Well said, son, well said. I believe you're the man who can get the job done. Now go on, son, and think on some more good things that will help the seed of the Negro mother." Momma Mamie and Rick were so excited about John's desire in running for mayor of New Orleans. They immediately started planning for his campaign. Momma Mamie started talking to some of her business associates who owned big businesses in the city. Because of their respect for her, they were willing to support her new nephew in running for the office. That next Sunday at church, he announced his desire in running for mayor of New Orleans; the church was behind him 100 percent. After all his work in running, with Rick standing right beside him, when the race was over, they announced that night that he had won by a landslide. Momma Mamie was at home listening to it on the radio. Rick was not only the first lady of the church, he was now the first lady of New Orleans. They had a beautiful life together; they would go to the city hall with all of the city officials. They were well-dressed on every occasion. The white women of the city couldn't believe that a black woman could have so much power and class about herself. Rick was always on the move; he and John went everywhere. On John's gospel meetings, preaching God's word, he was right by his side wherever he went. Through all the fame and traveling on the entire trip, Rick was still haunted by his secret. The more he listened to those powerful sermons preached by John, it began to prick his heart. It helped him see that what he had been doing was wrong, and he continued to ignore it, the lust that lined the core of her soul blinded by the veil of love. A couple of months later, while he and John was a way on a gospel meeting, they received a call at the hotel room from Momma Mamie's best friend, Erlean, stating that Momma Mamie had a bad stroke. Rick was so torn up about Momma Mamie's illness; it broke him down in tears.

He told John that he would have to rush back to New Orleans because Momma Mamie had a bad stroke, and that the doctor said he believes her body is to weak to recover from it. It was John's last night to preach in Los Angels. He asked Rick, "Do you want me to go with you to see about her?"

Rick said, "No, darling."

John said, "As soon as I finish, I will be right down there as soon as I can."

Rick took the first flight out to New Orleans. Once he got to the hospital, Joe was sitting outside of the door of the room, crying his little heart out. When he walked inside the room Momma Mamie was lying, Erlean was at her bedside with tears in the wells of her eyes. Erlean then walked out of the room to leave Momma Mamie and Rick alone to talk.

Once Momma Mamie felt his presence, she opened her eyes. "My darling baby boy, behind your camouflage of sin all these many years, I've still find love in the wall of my heart for you. You know, child, the Lord has blessed you and has protected your head dust for from the worse that lies in the blood that runs in your veins." Rick then began to cry.

Momma Mamie went on, "Child, wipe your eyes and stop crying. How are you, child?"

Rick then says, "In time, Momma, I will be fine. Everything is will be well with my soul."

"You know, child, your old Aunt Mamie knows you. You don't have to lie to me."

"I know, Momma."

"My body is tired, child. These old bones just don't work like they used to," Momma Mamie said, with a smile on her face. Rick began to cry even more to the point that his mascara began to run down his face.

Momma Mamie said unto him, "You know, baby honey child, a lady shouldn't spend her last days in a place like this, hon. I want you to take me home to that place where the legacy of the black madam began, hon, where a lady is supposed to die with dignity."

"Momma, don't go on talking like that, because you're going to be around for a long time. Do you hear me? Just stop it. You are breaking my heart into pieces." With tears falling from his eyes, he repeated, "Please, Momma, don't go on talking like that, talking about leaving me. You're just going to break my heart into pieces."

"Now, child, I believe my time is up. The good Lord up above is calling my name, and baby, when he calls your name, you got to move." She then laughed. "You know, child, it has always been in my prayer that the good Lord up above give you the time you need to get your soul ready for that great getting up morning. Like he did for Jezebel in the book of Revelations, but Jezebel did not want to follow the ways of the Lord. Because her heart was full of lust for this old sinful world, the Lord got tired of her evil ways because he saw that she was not going to change. He took her life from her and her blood. The dogs did lick it from the streets of the earth when she died. She never got the chance to ever repent of her sinful ways. In hell she shall lift up her eyes. I hope you repent before the Lord up above call your name, because I do not want you to have the same faith that Jezebel had. You know, child, on the other hand, I am proud of you and your happiness, child. I supported you because I did not want to push you away out there among the wolves of this bad world. All my life, I have lost the ones I loved to the wolves of this profane society in which we live. I said to my soul, child, I was not going to lose you to the trap of the curse of the madam. You know, child, sometime when a man allow his human wisdom guide him, he cannot see the truth sometime. Child, it's best to keep your opinion to yourself, when you force them on them sometime, it just pushing them further into their sins even more. Sometime, child, you just have to let the Lord guide them to rightness and hope it ain't to late. Baby, I would not tell you these things if I did not love you. I want you to know what you are doing is not right for your own soul in the eyesight of God. If I do not tell you these things, God will hold my soul accountable. Child, I got to tell you this because I've got to stand before him myself. I took a chance on my soul by supporting you in this great sin of yours because I love you so much, and I did not want you turn run away from me. You see, child, I hope that you change your ways before the good Lord above call your name like he is calling mine now. That man that you have deceived to marry him, God will not hold him encounter for this great sin that you have put on him. If you really love him, you will tell him the truth. Son, tell me something, will you give us a madam that will supersede the legacy of Momma Bea?"

"Yes, Momma, some way, somehow, I will give you a madam that will supersede the legacy of Momma Bea," Rick replied with tears in his eyes.

At that moment, Momma Mamie smiled, and Rick did not know what to do with himself. Momma Mamie then said, "Go now, child, and take your old Momma Mamie home." As he walked toward the door, Mamie said unto him, "Child, the Lord has had his hands around that man of yours. He has done no wrong. He do not know who you are and what is it that you are doing. You need now to study 'lhe holy word of God and found out what it is that He have plan for your life."

As he walked out the door of the room, to go and discharge her from the hospital, he could barely walk and see his way to the nurse's station, from the rain of tears that flooded his eyes. Rick told Joe that Momma Mamie wants to speak with him. "Come in. Momma Mamie is very weak." He got up from his chair and went into her bedside.

While Rick was at the nurse station filling out the discharge papers, Erlean, with tears in her eyes, rushed out of the room to the nursing station, where Rick was standing, and said unto him, "Come quickly!"

He dropped the clipboard he was holding and rushed down to the room where Momma Mamie was lying. Once he entered the room, he saw that Momma Mamie's eyes were closed. He then looked into the watery eyes of Joe holding her hand. Joe shook his head, letting him know that his dear friend has passed on. Rick then rushed to Momma Mamie's bedside and said unto her corpse, "No not now, Momma, not now. I need you, I need you. You cannot leave me now. We are going home." He was crying his heart out as he fell to the floor, on his knees, still holding her hand. "I promise, Momma, I will change. I promise I will change. Just speak to me please, Momma, just speak to me one more time. Please, Momma, please, Momma."

At that moment, John walked inside the room and lifted him from the floor and held him in his arms, saying to him, "Stop crying now. Everything is well with her soul. Everything will be okay."

Rick said unto him, "No, it's not. Can you see my momma is gone? What will I do? Who will I talk to now?"

"My rose, I am here. You can talk to me."

"You don't understand, you do not understand. My god, what have I done, what have I done?"

John then held him even closer to his chest, as Rick cried on his shoulder. At that moment, while Rick was crying on Reverend John's shoulder, he saw the Zulu witch slave walk through the room. Their eyes connected, and she vanished. The next Friday, Rick had put Momma Mamie's body on stake at her mansion for the people of the community to view her body before the funeral the next day. The funeral was the biggest in the city of New Orleans, cars were filled with flowers, and the funeral procession was long. One of Uncle Pittman old friends came down to do the eulogy. Also, one of her friends was a famous gospel singer who sang at her funeral; the song was, "No One Knows the Trouble I See." Rick's heart was broken. It was as if he had lost his best friend. That funeral was so big; it was as if they were burying a movie star. Momma Mamie was well loved by all who knew her. They took her to the graveyard to put her in that dark lonely grave far from everyone who loved her and respected her. Rick was so torn up inside, not only from the death of Momma Mamie, but also from the secret that lied in the pit of his soul. He looked at John as they sat near the coffin with the desire in her heart to tell him the truth, but the love of his heart kept the truth concealed inside his soul. After they left the gravesite, every one came back to the mansion for dinner, even Diamond was there to be by Rick's side, dressed in his woman attire. That night after everyone was gone, as John and Rick were getting ready for bed, Rick's conscience began to bother him again. He began to cry because of her memory of Momma Mamie and the fact that she was no longer there anymore. Once John realized he was crying, he came over where he was and held him inside his arms. At that moment, Rick's conscience was at ease because without a shadow of a doubt, he knew that John loved him like he had never been loved in his life. Because of this love experience, he was willing to continue on playing rush and roulette with his soul rather than tell John of his secret and take a chance on losing him forever. That night, he decided to keep that secret in the lonely tomb of his soul. The next day, John went to the office at the church after eating breakfast with Rick. As he got up from the table, he kissed him on the cheek, asking him if he would be all right.

Rick said, "I will be fine. Besides, I have to go and check on things at the company and meet with the board members to set things in order now that Momma Mamie's gone." Rick did not realize at this point that he was officially the new madam who will carry on the legacy of Momma Bea. After meeting with the board member of the company, in letting them know that there will be some new changes, now that he came back home. Once he got back inside the house, he laid his hat on the chair in the living room. He heard the phone ring. He call out for Joe to answer, but he did not hear it. He hurried to answer the phone only to find out that Momma Mamie's lawyer was on the on the other end. He said, "Hello, this is Madam Colleen speaking."

The lawyer said, "May I speak to Rick Smith please."

Rick said, "May I ask who is calling?"

He then said, "This Jimmy Moore, the Madam Mamie Pittman's lawyer. I am calling today in regard to her will."

"I am Rick Smith."

"I would like for you to come into my office and meet with you to talk about the will of Madam Mamie estate."

"When will you like for us to meet?"

"Thursday afternoon at twelve o'clock will be a good time."

"That will be fine, but first, I would like to meet you before the reading of the will."

"That will be finding. Thursday will be fine. I just want to talk to you about some more legal matters." He wanted to meet early with the lawyer because he did not want his identity to be exposed during its reading. He wanted the lawyer to refer to him as Madam Colleen rather Rick Smith.

Thursday morning came. Once he got into his office and knocked on the lawyer's door, he told him to come in. Mr. Jimmy stood up as if he knew who he was before he could say one word. Mr. Jimmy said, "Please have a seat, Madam Colleen.

Rick said, "How do you know my name?"

"Have a seat. It has been a long time since I last saw you. You were a small child. I see you have made some changes since then."

"I came in today because I notice that you ask for Rick Smith. As you can see, I have made some changes since the last time you have seen me."

"I am so sorry, Madam Colleen. Madam Mamie told me of your state some time ago. Please forgive me for I am an old man. Some time this old mind of mind slips me at time. As I was reading through the will, I noticed that Madam Mamie left all of her estate to you in the name of Rick Smith. Need not to worry, before she died, she told me of you and your state of transforming yourself into a woman. I just had forgotten. I understand your case. During the reading of the will, I will refer to you as Madam Colleen so we can keep your secret conceal. It will be up to you to keep this will out of the hands of anyone that do not know about your true identity."

Rick thanked Mr. Jimmy. "Your kindness will not be forgotten."

"I have been a friend of Madam Mamie for many years, and I plan to keep it that way, with the family as long as I can. I will meet you Thursday at the estate. Have Momma Mamie best friend there along with the butler. I must ask how Pussy Wussy is doing the dog."

"She is doing just fine." Rick smiled and walked out of the office, knowing that there would not be any links in his secret during the reading of the will.

When the reading of the will finally came around, it was now time for Madam Mamie's estate to be read. The lawyer arrived at the mansion at twelve o'clock sharp. Joe was standing on the side of the desk in the study quarters. Rick was sitting down in a chair in front of Madam Mamie's desk; John stood beside Rick. Once Mr. Jimmy enters inside the study quarters, where everybody was waiting, he took his seat in Momma Mamie's chair, behind her desk. He said unto them, "We have lost a wonderful lady and a dear friend of mine for many years." Tears began to fall from his eyes as he continued to speak, with a handkerchief in his hand, wiping the tears from his eye, saying with a whimpering voice, "She will truly be missed by all of us at C&B law firm. The will reads as following: I leave to my darling butler, Mr. Joe M. Butler, who have stuck by my side for so many years whom I loved so dear as a brother I did not have, whom I could tell anything to. It would stay between us like an iron nail driven into a steak of wood. His confidence was solid and trustworthy too. You baby honey child, I leave 2 million dollars for your safekeeping. And to my darling niece who will supersede the legacy and carry on the dream of the black madam, I leave you in full control of C&B Oil Company and 100 percent holder of all shares that lies in the company, all my beautiful hats and dresses and my Rolls-Royce Bentley, 60 million dollars in cash, 75 million in assets along with the mansion left to us by Momma Bea. Please take of my baby Pussy Wussy, my dog, until her time come, child. You are all she got not, child, and take care of yourself and look to the hill from which cometh your health. And remember, secrets will not last for they will come out someday. Love always, baby honey child, your Madam Mamie Bee Pittman. To my best friend, Erlean, I leave my shoes and 1 million dollars."

After the reading the will, they enjoyed a sumptuous feast that Rick prepared for all of them, and together, they embraced the new dawn.

Chapter 27

Ten years later, Rick was not his usual self, haunted by his secret and thinking about the words that Momma Mamie spoke unto him before she died.

John asked him, "Is everything okay, my darling lily?"

Rick responded, "Everything is well. I'm just thinking about all the things that I have to do today. I have a little shopping at the supermarket and take care of a few things for the company, honey. I'll just be fine. Run along and take care of the Lord's business."

Once John left for work, Rick began getting dressed to go shopping. He had Joe bring the car around. During his day of shopping, he saw someone who looked familiar, someone he had not seen in many years, so he began to stare at the mysterious-looking woman. He moved closer to get a good look at who the woman was. Once he got closer, he realized it was a face that he knew her in high school years—his ex-girlfriend Tamarra. He paused in motion with devastation rushing through his heart, wondering if he should turn around or walk away, leaving the suspense of knowing the new ideas that lied in the center of his current reality. Because of the ancient memory that lied within his soul, he could not turn away because he knew within himself that the love that he had still dwell within his being, which provoked him to overlook his tears, to gaze her presence once more. He continued pushing his buggy full of groceries closer to her, still camouflaged as a woman. Speechless in knowing what to say before he could convey the question, Tamarra automatically recognized his hidden identity as being the First Lady of New Orleans. As Rick approached closer, when he looked into Tamarra's eyes, tears began to fill the wells of his eyes. When he looked at her, he noticed that she was still the same girl, but she aged a little.

Tamarra said unto him, "Are you the major wife?" Before he could say anything, she said, "It's a great honor to meet you. I admire you so much."

Rick asked, "Madam, may I ask your name?"

"I am so sorry. My name is Tamarra. You are Momma Mamie's niece.

"Yes, I am."

"I never knew of her ever having a niece, only a nephew name Ricky Smith. It has been a long time since I have talked to him. Have you heard from him?"

"Yes, a couple of months ago."

"Do you have a number where I can contact him?"

"No, I do not, but if he calls, I will tell him that you are looking for him. One thing I do know is that he is doing well. The late time I heard he leaved in Miami.

"Well, how is Momma Mamie?

"She passed about ten years ago."

"I am sorry to hear that. I did not know. Did Rick come down for the funeral?"

"Yes, he did."

"Here is my number. If he every calls, tell him that I have something very important to tell him.

"Is there anything I can help you with?"

"No, I just need to talk to him. If you ever get in touch with him, let him know that I need to talk with him."

"How have you been?"

"I have been doing well. I live in Los Angels with my husband and my daughter, Elaine."

"What bring you back to New Orleans?"

"I came to visit my mother."

Because of Rick's desire wanting to spend more time with her, to see what it was she had been doing all these many years and to find out what it was that she had to talk to him about, he asked her, "So tell, how long you are planning to stay in New Orleans?"

"For a couple more days."

"Say, how would you like to hang out with the mayor's wife before you leave? Maybe we could have lunch or something?"

"I would like that very much."

"How is your mother?"

"She is not doing well. She has been very sick these past few years. I had to put her in a home care because I was unable to take care of her."

"I am sorry to hear that. I did not know. Where is your daughter?"

"She is here with me in New Orleans at my mother's house."

"How old is she?"

"She is thirty years old and married."

"You must have had her right after you got out of high school?"

"Yes, I did."

Rick said, "How does Friday sound? My husband will be leaving to go out town for business. That will gives some time to myself."

"That will be great!"

"That will be fine. I will have my driver pick you on Friday afternoon at six o'clock. We will go to one of my favorite restaurants in town New Orleans."

"That will be great, is not every day you do not get the chance to hang out with the mayor's wife."

"Think nothing of it. If you are a friend of Rick's, you a friend of mine. I will see you tomorrow."

"Okay, by." Tamarra waved as she walked off, leaving Rick in deep thought. When John got in from the office, Rick was sitting in the study, in a deep thought about his encounter with Tamarra, wondering in his mind what it was that she had to tell him. Once he entered inside the house and noticed Rick, John knew that he had something heavy on her mind. He walked inside the room where he was sitting and asked, "Is everything okay?"

Rick said, "Darling, everything is just fine. I just have a lot on my mind, nothing that you need to worry yourself about."

"Do you want to talk about it?"

"It really nothing. I am just sitting here thinking about my momma and fulfilling the shoes of the black madam." That was not the only thing he was thinking about, in his mind, he had remembered the conversation that he and Tamarra had at the supermarket that afternoon.

John said, "You will have no problem in filling the shoes of the black madam, because you are the essence of a woman and a very extremely beautiful one." At that moment, John gave him a kiss on the forehead.

"I think you, you are the best man that a madam can every dream of having."

"So tell me how your day went." John took his seat to listen to Rick.

"I had a very interesting day. I ran into and old friend of mine that I have not seen in over thirty years at the shopping market today."

"Well, did you invite her over for dinner?"

"No, I didn't, but I invited her out to dinner on Friday afternoon."

"I hate that I will not get the chance to meet your friend. I will be out town on tomorrow afternoon. Maybe that will be great. You hang out with your old friend. Does she live her in New Orleans?"

"No, she stays in Los Angels. She said she is here to see her mother because she is quite ill."

"I wish she stayed her so you would have some other friend to hang out with other so other getting caught up in your work and your ladies' organization. I have noticed that you do not have any close friends."

"Some times when a lady is in love, in their heart, they feel that the only friend that they need is the person of whom they are in love with."

"That is a wonderful way to feel. By the way, I will be leaving a little early for the preacher conference."

"Darling, when will you be leaving?"

"The first thing in the morning, if you would like, you can go with me so that you can get out of the house and keep me company."

"That's okay, darling. I will be just fine. Beside, I have a dinner date with an old best friend of mine tomorrow. This will a great time for us to catch on old times."

"That would be great, but if you decide to change your mind, let me know. I tell you what, by it being I will be leaving out town early on tomorrow, let's take stroll out on the river and spend some time together this afternoon."

That afternoon, John and Rick took a walk by the riverside. While they were walking, John said unto Rick, "I have noticed since Aunt Mamie died, you have not been acting the same. My fair beautiful doll, please tell me what it is that troubles your soul."

"There is nothing wrong. I'm just been missing Momma Mamie's here lately. There is nothing for you to worry your little heart about," Rick said unto him, knowing in his heart that he had a cloud of burden to pour out like that of the rain ready to drop from the clouds of his dark and weary mind. "You know what? Everything that is troubling my soul, the word of my mind cannot truly identify it and with to allow me to convey it unto you. Everything is still okay because I have you right here by my side."

As they continued walking, John held her hand and sang a song, "A Shelter in the Time of Storm." It was as if he knew that there was something within Rick's heart that was eating him alive; he just didn't know what. As they continued to walk, John said unto him, "You know, baby, I've been thinking about me and you talking a road trip somewhere just to get away from New Orleans."

Rick said, "That sounds like fun. Where?"

John said, "I don't know yet, but I will think on it. We will talk about it more when I get back from this trip."

That next morning, John left for Washington, DC, to attend the governors' conference. On that same afternoon, Rick and Martha had their dinner date. He called her on the phone and told her he would pick her up at 6:00 p.m. Rick had Joe get Momma Mamie's car ready to drive him down, to pick her up. When he arrived at her mother's house, it was like the old days, only her father didn't answer the door. Joe knocked on the door. Once she answered, Joe said, "The madam is waiting. It good to see you, Mrs. Tamarra. It has been a long time."

Tamarra said, "Yes, it has. It is good to see you again too."

They then walked toward the car. Joe opened the car door for her and let her inside. Tamarra said unto Rick, "I remember this car when I was in high school. Mrs. Mamie would let Rick come and pick me up in this same car."

"Oh, really? Momma Mamie took really good care of this car while she was alive." When they arrived at the restaurant, they were seated.

Rick said, "So tell me, what type of work you do."

Tamarra said, "I am a nurse. I've been a nurse for over twenty years. You know when I was dating your cousin, Rick, he never mentioned that he had a cousin."

Rick then laughed. "That Rick never thinks. Maybe it's just, I never crossed his mind."

"Maybe that was the case. So tell me something, all these years, you nor Momma Mamie really keep any contact with him."

"Since our college years, Rick closed himself off from the world in which he knew. I have you to know that Rick is still alive and well somewhere, and enough about Rick.

For now, tell me a little about you and your family. You are married?

Tamarra then responded, "Yes, I am. I have been married for ten years. You know, Madam Colleen, when I had finished college, me and Elaine moved to Los Angels, California."

"Elaine? Who is that?"

"That's my daughter."

"Oh your daughter."

"Once we moved there, I meet and married Michael. He is a doctor."

"Who is the poor child's father?"

"The whole reason it is important that I need to talk to Rick because he is her father."

Rick couldn't believe the words he heard come from Tamarra's mouth. Joe was eating dinner with them that day, and he almost choked on a chicken bone. Rick nearly passed out on the spot.

Rick said, "By all means, this is a shock to me. We didn't know. Will excuse me for a moment? I need to go to the ladies' room."

Joe said unto him, "Madam Colleen, must I assist you?"

Rick said, "There is no need. I will be just fine."

Once Rick walked off from the table, Tamarra said, "I did not mean to upset her."

Joe said, "The madam is not upset. She is just caught in a state of shock."

Once Rick got inside restroom, he began crying, because he could not believe that he had a child, wondering inside his mind what he will do. He caught a hold of himself, wiped his eyes, and then walked back to the table where he was sitting. Once he got back to the dinner, Joe stood and pulled his seat out for him to be seated.

Tamarra asked, "Are you okay, Madam Colleen?"

Rick said, "I will be fine. This news just caught me by surprise that all. May I ask you a question?"

"Go right ahead."

"Why is it that you have kept this from the family all these many years?"

"I was so ashamed of having this baby out of wedlock. I just could tell Momma Mamie of this. I decided to take my baby away with me and raise her myself, because I felt Rick was not in love with me like I was in love with him. It haunted me for many years that I don't try to contact him to let him know that he had a daughter, but I could not find him." She then reached inside her purse and pulled out a picture of Elaine and showed it to Rick. Once he looked at the picture, he began to cry. She looked like Rick and his mother, Lorene.

Tamarra then asked, "Madam Colleen, are you all right?"

Rick then said, "I will be just fine. It just all this news just got me worked up that's all. Continue on, never mind me."

"Ever since Elaine was a small child, she asked of her father what was he like. I would tell her he was the love of my life. He was a great gentleman. He was very sweet and very good-looking."

After dinner that night, as they approached Tamarra's mother's house, when they pulled inside the driveway, Rick asked, "When will you be leaving?"

She said, "I will be leaving the day after tomorrow."

"I would really like to meet the child before you leave New Orleans."

"That will be fine. Elaine would like that because she have asked me many time about her father and his family."

"I would like for you and her to come to my home on tomorrow afternoon for dinner. I will have the butler pick you up tomorrow afternoon around five o'clock."

"I will let her know. I know she will be excited to finally me some of her father's family members."

"I cannot wait to meet her. I just know she have her grandmother eyes."

On their way home, Joe asked Rick, "Madam Colleen. what will you ever do?

Rick said, "I do not know, I do not know." At that moment, he knew within his lonely soul that he must do something but did not know what. But one thing he did know was that she was really the mirror of his soul. His heart was very troubled.

The next night, Joe went over to pick them up while Rick was waiting at the mansion. Lady, the maid, prepared a beautiful dinner. While Rick was waiting, he paced the floor backward and forward until he heard the wheels of the car drive up on the pavement of the driveway. He rushed back into the living quarters of the house and waited until they approached the door. He then thought to himself, *If only Momma Mamie was here. She would know exactly what to do in a case like this.* He then said aloud to herself, "Catch a whole to yourself, Madam Colleen. Everything will be just fine." When Tamarra and his unknown mirror approached the doors of her new destiny, Rick's heart began to rush like that of a mighty, rushing wind. Joe called for him and announced their presence.

When he walked into the room where the both of them were standing, he looked into Elaine's eyes and saw a look that he thought was lost forever—the look that he had camouflaged. Also, she looked just like her mother, Lorene. As they continued to look at one another, tears began to fill their eyes. They both stood speechless, as he began to approach closer to her. Not knowing what to do or how to respond, she began to walk forward toward him. The tears that flowed from Elaine's eyes were tears of happiness because she had finally connected with a life she had never known, a life that she had dreamed of having. She was like a child who had long waited for her father to bring a treasure that she could open—after the many years that passed between them both, once their long-apart lives connected again, once their chest and arms embraced each other. At that moment, Rick felt like he wasn't alone anymore. Tamarra at that moment had a smile with tears in her eyes, to know that her daughter finally met her family members. Elaine finally said, "It is a great to meet you, Madam Colleen."

Rick said unto her, "I am happy for you to be in my presence. I did not know that you existed."

Joe then told them dinner is ready. Once they were seated, Elaine asked Rick, who was dressed in his beautiful woman attire, "Is it okay if I call you Aunt Colleen?"

Rick said, "Child, you can call me whatever you want to call me."

"Aunt Colleen, for many year, it has been my desire to meet my father. Mother has tried a few time in trying to find him, but we have not had any luck in doing so. Do you know any idea where we could find him I so long to see him?"

"Baby honey child, your father is somewhere hiding from all those that he loves. He is not far, he just waited on a good reason to come back out from his bondage."

"Tell me, Aunt Colleen, why is it that he is hiding?"

"Sometime, people do this, and they really don't know why. Maybe he would not have went into hiding if he knew that you were here. One day, he will be able to answer these questions for you. There is one thing I am very sure of is that he loves you with all his heart. Madam Elaine, I promise you one day, you will see him."

"When can I see him when?" There was excitement all over Elaine's face.

"Soon but I first have to work out a few things in finding him again."

Elaine then looked at her mother, happy, with tears in her eyes, with hope inside of her soul. She then asked, "Aunt Colleen, what type of person it he?"

Rick said, "He a very gentle man, a man who love to play tennis, very sweet and kind. Your father, child, went into hiding far from the world and reality that he knew chasing after something that he found, but soon or later, he realized that the treasure in which he found was not the life for him. He hid his face from the one he truly loved, and I see that person is you," Tears began to fall from his eyes. "That's enough about Rick for now. We have plenty of time to talk about him. Tell me a little about you."

Elaine said, "I went to Moore House University and study in business management and economics and received my four-year degree. I now work for J. P. Morgan Bank as an accountant. I don't have any children. One day, it is my hope to get married and have some children. It is my hope that one day, I will get the chance to come back and spend some time with you and learned more about my father and hopefully find him."

"That will be great. I will like that so very much." He then looked over at Tamarra; he noticed she had tears in her eyes. He did not know whether she was crying because of the excitement by it being that his mirror had finally seen her reflection or because she has finally found what she had been looking for, for so many years. This day was the happiest day of his life, to know that there was something in this world that looked something like him.

After dinner that night, they all hugged each other. He then told Joe to take them home. Once the car was brought around to front of the house, Tamarra looked in his eyes, as if she knew who he was. He then shut that out of his mind, thinking to himself she couldn't possibly know. When their ride was ready, he walked them to the car. Joe let Elaine into the car first, but before she entered inside, she said unto him, "Thanks, Aunt Colleen, for spending time with me and sharing with her some things about my father. You have made me really happy. I will be calling you really soon."

"I will look forward to you calling. I will be sending for you so I can tell you all you need to know about your family history and your father."

She smiled and entered the car. Tamarra then gave Rick a hug and a kiss on the cheek. She then whispered in his ear, "Good-bye, Rick. I thank you for spending this time with me and our daughter. I want you to know that I will not mention anything to her about you. I will let you tell her in your own way."

At that moment, Rick almost fainted. He could not believe she actually knew who he was even if he was dressed like a women. He then in turned and asked her softly, "How is it that you know?"

As she was entering the car, she said, "I never forgot a smile. It was all inside your eyes."

"I did not know that. I did not know."

"I know. Never mind now. You have a daughter now, help her rid herself of the empty void that lies inside her soul. She really want to meet you."

At that moment, tears started to fall from his eyes. "Tamarra, I did not want you to find out this way."

Tamarra said, "Stop crying. There is one thing that I want you to know and is I never stop loving you. You will be just fine. Elaine is waiting. I must go now. Take care of yourself. Good-bye." She gave him a kiss on the cheek and got inside the car and the driver left.

When he walked back inside house, Rick looked up at the wall at Momma Mamie's and Momma Bea's portraits. "Them I have finally given unto your as madam that will supersede the legacy of the black madam."

Chapter 28

The next morning, John called him to see how he was doing. He told John everything is well within his soul. John then asked him, "Would you like to come to Washington? I would be staying a couple more days than expected. I have been invited to a banquet. I would will like for you to come down and be a part of it with me on this occasion. A lot of the governor's wife will be with her husbands. I would like for them to meet for first time to see what the southern bell of New Orleans look like. I have talked to couple of my friends about the programs that you had set up for raising money for black youth to go to college. They want to hear about your program."

Rick said, "I would love to come down and spend some time with you and meet some of your friends."

"I will put together a speech for the ball. Maybe you will get some more supporters for your programs."

"I will be leaving out the first thing in the morning."

The next day, Rick left for Washington, to meet John. He already went shopping for a new dress and hat and shoes to match so that those people in Washington could see what the first lady of New Orleans was working with. He and Sister Mary, one of his friends from the church, pick the dress and shoes up from the dress shop the day before her flight leaves.

When he arrived in the airport of Washington, DC, John was standing inside with an arm full of roses, waiting for him to get off the plane. Once they left the airport, they went and had dinner. Rick's mind spent days thinking about his daughter, Elaine. Rick wanted so badly to tell John of his new discovery, but he thought that he would not understand, and his secret would he exposed. He didn't want to take risk losing the love of his life, so he decided to keep it to himself. He knew in his soul that he had to do something but did not know what.

In John's mind, he knew that there was something wrong with him, but he didn't know what. John said, "Madam, is there something wrong?"

"Oh, is nothing have you order yet?" Rick was very happy to see him of course, but the secret that lied in the back of his mind was eating him inside. He felt at this moment in his life that he was now trapped in between two worlds, the world in which he loved so well, even though he knew that it was not the right reality that he needed. He was far too deep to turn around from it, so she prayed to the good Lord to help him make the right decision.

Rick said to himself, *Enough of this thinking. Let me enjoy this moment while it lasts with the love of my life.*

While they were eating their lunch, John asked, "How have you been doing while I was away?"

Rick said, "I had a wonderful time with my old friend. She told me that they both came over to the mansion for dinner. We talked about me coming to California to visit them."

"That great! You need to get away. Have you gotten your speech together for the ball tonight?"

"I am still working on it. It's almost finished."

"I cannot wait to hear what it is that you have to say. They couldn't wait to meet you. I just know you are going to do a great job in convincing them to help push for those black kids dreams for higher education."

After they finished eating their lunch, both of them went to the hotel. Rick worked on his speech. Once it was time for them to go to the ball, they began getting dressed. Once Rick was dressed, John entered inside the room where he was. Rick said unto him, "How do I look?"

John stood there in amazement and said, "Darling, you look great. You will be the most beautiful and best dressed lady of the afternoon."

Rick sat down on the bed and told John to come sit down next to him as she patted the bed, signaling to him where she wanted him to sit. Once he took his seat next to him, Rick then began to rub him on his back, telling him how much he appreciates him for being the man that he is. Rick then said, "I must tell you are a great preacher and mayor. You having been doing great job. Mount Zion Baptist Church and the city of New Orleans could not have pick a better man for the job. I want you to know that I have great respect for you, and I love you with all my heart."

John said to him, "Madam Colleen, I have you to know that I have been thinking about the up and coming election, and I have decided that during the next term, I will not be running." "Why? You have been doing a great job."

"Well, I been thinking I have been spending too much time away from the church and you. Preaching is something that I really love doing. I just think that's where I am needed most, and I am very so much in love with you. I just feel I need to spend as much time with you as much as I can."

"Whatever you decide to do, I want you to know that I am behind you a hundred percent of the way."

They kissed and hugged each other. John said unto Rick, "I figure once we get back home, we will take that relaxing trip I talk to you about. That trip will allow us to get away from everything so we can spend some quiet time together, just me and you."

"Honey, I would like that a great deal. Where will we go?"

"Not too far, some place close nice and relaxing. Don't' worry about that. I want to surprise you. I will tell you this, it is somewhere I found to be one of my favorite places out the outside of New Orleans city."

"You never mention it to me before."

"I was waiting for the right moment."

"Oh really."

"Yes, I just knew you will like it."

"Let me help you with your tie." He then helped John put on his jacket. They headed out to the ballroom inside the hotel. Rick thought, *If only Momma Mamie could see me now.* Even though his mind was heavy, he realized he had to be at his best for his darling husband on that special night and give a pretty good speech that would represent the city of New Orleans and her as the first lady, hoping that she would raise money to help the young underprivileged children go to college.

When he and John walked inside the ballroom, everyone was standing around, drinking wine in their expensive wine glass. Once they realized that Major Adams and the First Lady of New Orleans were walking through the door, everyone became motionless. They acted as if they had never seen such a beautiful woman like him before, with the character that she portrayed.

"I must say, Momma Colleen, you are extremely beautiful," one gentleman said and kissed her hand.

Rick's hair was up in a bonnet ball; he had on the most beautiful red dress you have ever seen. All the ladies and their husband swept around him like bees. Because of his beauty, they were trying to know who this southern bell dressed in red is. His purpose was to give a great impression and give his speech to raise money to assure that the African children would have a chance to reach equality through the lifeline of education. The ladies who were standing around him had told him that they had heard of the great things he had been doing in New Orleans. In their black community for the underprivileged children, they asked him, "How do you manage to be a preacher's wife and a mayor's wife? Where do you find the time?"

Rick said, "The energy that come from the love of my husband enable me to do so, my darlings. If it wasn't for him and God, I would not know how it would get done."

That afternoon, everything was so beautiful. The setting of the ballroom was of a red velvet and gold trim, and all the man were dressed in black tuxedos with white shirts and white bow ties, walking around in the lobby area of the banquet hall, waiting patiently until the program started. John and Rick were the only blacks there; they were the center of the afternoon that night. They were placed at their assigned seats, together with Governor Patterson and Governor Richardson and their wives. Their wives were shocked from how beautiful Rick was and how he responded so intelligently to their questions. They were shocked that a black woman like him could have so much influence and power. Once the ladies saw that there was no break in his flow of conversation, they began to ask insulting questions, trying to insult his intelligence. Rick answered their question in a very savvy way with a plight smile, letting them know that if you are going to challenge me, you better do a little more study on the subject. Once he answered the question, John alone was amazed, but not as much as the others who sat at the table. He already knew that his wife could handle any situation that came her way with style and class. Once dinner was announced, everyone went to their assigned places to be served. Once dinner was served and everyone ate, the chairman of the board got up and started the programs for that afternoon.

After his amazing speech, it was so amazing and moving that everyone gave him a standing ovation. After the program was over, a lot of the governors' wives approached him with their business cards, asked if they could be apart of his Elite Women's Club because they want to help him raise money for the student in America, who could not afford to go to college—some even gave her checks. After the speech, the next year, he raised over a hundred thousand dollars for the Momma Bea College fund. He had enough money to help twenty thousand students go to college the next following year.

That next day after the dinner party, he and John flew back to New Orleans. When they got back that afternoon, John had a surprise for him. Rick didn't know anything about it. Once they got inside the house, Rick noticed that the lights were dim, and flowers were everywhere. The table was sat with a snow-white table clothes candles were on the table lit.

Joe was standing at the table. "Dinner is ready."

John pulled out Rick's chair, for him to be seated, and pushed him up to the table. Then John kissed him on the cheek, and he took his seat. As they began eating, John said to Rick, "Madam Colleen, I am very lucky as a man to have you as my wife. All my life, my heart has desired a reflecting image of you in the back of his mind, when it came to the ideal characteristics of a lady. There is no greater woman that God could have created for a little o' man like."

In the back of Rick's mind, he thought, *My darling, me man the man of whom I desire with all my heart if only you know of my secret.*

Rick said, "My darling gentleman, since the youth of my soul, I too have dreamed of you too. In the reality of my darkness, I've seen a shadow of your countenance. But I just couldn't see the handsome face of my love to attach a name to your present. Not knowing that it was you all the time, and now here you are in the life that I have yearned for all my life."

"I have something to give you." John got up and went to the drawer and pulled out a red velvet box with a red bow around it. He handed it to him. He opened it, and it was the most beautiful diamond ring and necklace and earrings his eyes had ever seen. His heart melted. He then began to cry with excitement in his heart. He then stood up from his seat and rushed over to the other side of the table, where he was sitting, and gave him the biggest hug and kiss that he could ever give.

The next morning when they awoke, John told Rick, "Get up. We are going to take a drive."

"Where are we going?"

"Don't worry, I have something to show you. it's one my favorite places."

"What do I need to wear?"

Just put on anything. You are beautiful anyway. Hurry, we must go."

Rick rushed and put on a beautiful white dress and one of her white sun hats. Once he was ready, they got into the car and left. Once they arrived at John's favorite place for meditation, Rick was amazed, seeing the beautiful grass. "Baby, this place is beautiful. Why haven't you brought me here before?"

John said, "I was waiting for the right moment."

The reason John brought Rick to his favorite place was that he felt that there was something that was disturbing him, and he just didn't know what. He brought him there to express his love to him and to let him know that he would be there for him no matter what. As they walked along the bank of the river, they decided that they would sit down along the bank and look out over the water and enjoy the cool breeze.

Then John said to Rick, "You know, Madam Colleen, I want you to know that you are the most beautiful lady that a man can meet in one lifetime. The love that I have for you words cannot define. When I began to think how it is that I feel, the adjectives throws their hand up in retreat. One can express my ideas of love for you better then William

Shakespeare when he wrote the poem 'Shall I Compare Thee to a Summer's Day?' May I?"

Rick nodded his head and said, "Yes, you may."

John began to quote the words of Williams Shakespeare:

> Shall I compare thee to a summer's day? Thou art more lovely and more temperate: Rough winds do shake the darling buds of may and summer's lease hath all too short a date: Sometime too hot the eye of heaven shines, And often his gold complexion dimmed; and every fair sometime declines, By chance, or nature's changing course, untrimmed; But they eternal summer shall not fade, Nor loose possession of that fair thou ow'st, Nor shall death brag thou wand'rest in his shade, when in eternal lines to time thou grow'st. So long as men can breathe or eyes can see, so long lives this, and this gives life to thee.

Tears began to fall from John's eyes. Rick then began to quote a poem by Michael Drayton entitled "Since There's No Help."

> Since there's no help, come let us kiss and part. Nay, I have done, you get no more of me; And I am glad, yea glad with all my heart, That thus so cleanly I myself can free. Shake hands for ever, cancel all our vows, and when we meet at any time again, Be it not seen in either if our brows That we one out of former love retain. Now at the last grasp of Love's latest breath, When Faith is kneeling by his bed or death, and Innocence is closing up his eyes—now if thou wouldst when all have given him over, From death to life thou might'st him recover!

Once he finished saying the quote, tears also filled Rick's eyes because he remembered all the hurt that he had been through in his past, in his quest to find love, through the drugs and the abuse. At this moment, he now realized that he had finally found the man who gives him hope again, when he almost gave up on love. Once the quote was finished, Rick looked deep into John's eyes, and said, "Before I meet you, my darling love, I asked myself, is this God desire that the human tongue calls love? Is it now ready to take it last breath and die within me and that lied in my heart screamed yes. But when our eyes connected, I said to my very soul on that day, now if thou wouldst, when all have giving over from death to life thou might'st I yet recover. At that moment when the pulse of my heart was pumping slow, you came along and helped me recover." He hugged John and slowly whispered in his ear, as the tears dripped from his eyes, "You are the greatest creation the world has ever known."

Once they left the park, as they were driving on that evening on their way home, they saw a black family who were broken down on the side of the road. The family was a very poor family. The father was a very big man who had shoes with holes in them with ragged overalls on. His wife was sitting inside the truck with four little children, one teenage boy who was outside helping his father fix something underneath the hood of the truck. Rick noticed them and said unto John, "Look at those poor people." John decided to turn around to help them. Once John got out of the car, he asked, "Is there anything I can help you with?" T

he big husky man said with a deep voice, "We'ze broke down. Iz been working and working on this truck for some time now and Iz just can't get it to crank."

John asked, "Where are you from?"

"We'ze from Water Valley, Mississippi. We'ze Baptist and Holy Ghost filled people."

John then smiled to know that someone else love the Lord like he did and also from the excitement that the man expressed in knowing Jesus. John said, "I tell you what, let's get you and your family off the road. I live about ten miles down the road. What you say y'all all jump in the car and let's go to my house and I get my auto man to get your truck towed into his shop so he can see if he can find out what's wrong with it. I want you to meet my wife." He then walked to the car to let Madam Colleen out so she could meet the family. Once they got into the car, he opened the door and reached inside his jacket pocket and pulled out a snow-white hanky and put it down on the ground for Rick to step out of the car on. When Rick got out of the car, he and John walked up to the big tall man and the little boy. John said, "I introduce you my wife and the First Lady of New Orleans, Madam Colleen.

Rick then said, "It is an honor to meet you all. Let's get out of this hot weather and go to a place where you fine people can cool off."

They all got out of the truck. Rick picked up one of the little girls out of the backseat and toted her to the car. The mother got the other two little girls and followed closely behind the husky man and his son sat in the front seat. Once they arrived at the mansion, one of the girls said, "This is the most beautiful lest house I have ever seen."

Rick said, "I said the same thing, child, when I saw it for the first time."

Once they got to the front door, Joe opened the door to let them in. Rick said unto him, "Get something together for these fine people eat and make right the restrooms so they can freshen up. I also wanted you to get all of there side, and I can get some clothing brought from Mrs. Ashley over here for them."

The man said, "Madam, you don't have to do that. We will be just fine."

Rick said, "I insist. Baby, if you have been through the things I've been through, you would understand. Besides, God would not had any other way. I believe since he has blessed me, I should bless someone else with the blessing that he has given me."

The husky man's wife said, "Hush, James, let God bless us. Don't stand in the way of God blessing. Mrs. Colleen, you have a mighty fine house."

"Why thank you, Mrs. Shirley. It was given to me from my grandmother, Momma Bea."

Joe got everything ready for them to freshen up. He came downstairs and said, "Everything is ready for you all to freshen up with. Right this way." He showed them to the bathroom and to the room where they would be sleeping. While they were in the shower, Rick's clothing store delivered their clothes. They got dressed and ate dinner.

John said unto the man after eating dinner, "Let's say you and me walk around the place, and I will show you the highlights of the landscape around the house."

Rick said to James's wife, "That's great. We can go and sit out on the desk and have some lady talk while the Children run around and play." She then had the maid to go upstairs and get some of her balls so that the children could play with.

As John and the man walked around the landscape of the mansion, John said, "So tell me a little about yourself."

The man said, "We'ze from a little town called...down in Mississippi. I'ze a preacher of a little holy ghost filled church down there. It's not much of a church building. We'ze poe' folk, but when we'ze having church, we praise the Lord like you never believe."

John began to laugh. "Preacher, what brings you to these parts?"

"My wife only sister died of cancer, and she was s her only living family member. We spend all our money to come down and make sure her sister was buried. Well, she'ze been really taken it hard. She'ze been quiet for two week, not really saying anything, until she got her, I figure once I got her back home, she will be just fine."

While they were walking and talking, Rick and the man's wife we're also having a talk.

Rick said unto the lady, "Honey, you don't talk much."

"There nothing much to talk about," she replied, as she continued to look out over the beautiful lawn in a daze. Once the lady spoke these words, Rick knew that something was wrong. She said unto Rick, "The place you have here for yourself. I once had something as beautiful that no house or beautiful garden could ever compare to. That was my sister, my only sister of whom the good Lord took away from me. Now that she's gone, the beautiful world that I knew has turn into darkness, and now I have nothing to talk about."

Rick realized that the life of Momma Mamie was the beauty of his life and it was really gloomy when she passed away. He then said, "I understand what it is that you are going through. If I could, I would give all this up to just have one more moment with my Momma Mamie. You are right. There is something more beautiful than materialistic things in this world and that the life of someone that you truly love. Once that is gone, nothing really matters anymore. But God has blessed me with the man of my dreams."

"The devil will also bless you with something, and some folks don't realize it because of the sin that lies inside their soul."

They then both looked out over the lawn in daze in silence. That night, when everyone was in bed, Rick and John had a conversation.

John said, "You know, these people are really good people. There must be something we can do for them. You know, I found out today that he is a preacher of some small church in Mississippi."

Rick said, "I know. I had a long talk with his wife. I found out that she is really grieving over the lost of her sister. You know, we have a lot of money. They really need some things. Let's give them some help so they can have a new beginning."

"That's a great idea. You know, the Bible says it's more bless it to give then to receive. Let's give them some money to rebuild that church, and maybe one day we can go and visit them to see the progress that they have made some time in the near future. How much do you think we should give?"

"One day, the children hopeful will go to college. They probably need some work done on their home and some new clothes. Let's say we give them twenty-five thousand dollars, fifteen thousand in a check for rebuilding of their church, and ten thousand for themselves. Maybe you can talk to the man at the church about sending him a salary every week to help him preach the word of God."

"That's a great idea. I will call the bank the first thing in the morning to bring over five thousand dollars in cash in the morning, and we will write out a check for the rest before our guest live. That way, they will have money to travel with."

The next morning while they were eating breakfast, the man said unto John, "Have you heard from the truck? We'ze got to get back to see about our home."

John said, "He will be calling anytime to let me know if it's ready."

"We'ze show glad, and we'ze thank you and your fine wife for letting us stay the night with you fine people."

John said, "We have enjoyed having you here with us. Anytime when every you pass through these parts again, feel free to stop by again because our home is your home."

Once he made this statement, Joe came into the dining quarters. "Sir John, the auto man is on the phone."

John then dropped his napkin on the table. "Excuse me." He then went to answer the phone. The auto man told him that the motor inside the truck was shot, and he can't repair it. John then called Madam Colleen in to the phone area and told her what the auto man said about the truck. John said he was thinking that they should get them another truck, and Rick agreed. John called the local car dealership and orders a 1957 Chevy truck. He then told the car dealer to send it right over, and that he would do the paper work later on the afternoon, so the car was delivered to their house. The family had no idea what was going on. Once they sat, everything was in order for their trip. They went back into the dining area, where they were sitting, eating breakfast. The man asked, "Is everything okay with the truck?"

John said, "The auto man said that the truck motor was shot, and that he could not repair it." It shook them both, the husband and the wife. John said, "Need not to worry, the Lord has provided a way for me and my wife to give you some transportation to get back to your home safely. It will be here shortly."

The man said, "We don't know how to thank you."

John said, "Me and my wife have a gift for you. Here is some money to help you rebuild that church building and give you some traveling money to get back to your home." At that that time, John called Joe who brought in the money and check in a silver tray. He opened it and gave the check to the man and said, "This money is for the rebuilding of God kingdom. Maybe one day, me and my wife will come down and visit you and see the work you have done on it."

Once the man and his wife looked at the check, they were surprised. The check was written for 15 thousand dollars. The man almost choked on the egg that he was eating.

Then John said, "Here is five thousand dollars cash for your traveling expensive." The man had never seen that much money before in his life and neither his wife. He then pushed his chair away from the table and fell down on his knees and began to pray, thanking the Lord for the blessing that he had sent to him. He then began to cry with joy inside his heart. Once they were ready to go, when they walked outside, they notice a brand-new truck parked outside.

John said, "The Bible says it is more bless it to give that receive. The Lord has bless you with this new car."

They both were amazed. Then one of the little girls said, with tears in her eyes, "May God bless you both." All of them had tears of joy. Then they all got into the truck and drove off. They waved bye to John and Rick. John and Rick, with the maid and the butler, waved good-bye as well, with smiles on their faces.

Chapter 29

Later on that day, John said unto Rick, "Let's say we get the ranch hand to get the horses ready for us to take a ride."

Rick said, "That sound like a great idea."

They took a ride for over half of the day on Momma Bea's one hundred acres of land. They stopped the horses, as they looked over the property. John asked Rick, "Who will we leave all this to after we are died and gone since you don't have any more living relatives and neither one of us have any children."

"Don't you have nieces and nephews living?" Rick took off his hat.

John said, "Yes I do, but I am talking about the legacy of Momma Bea. Who will you leave your part to?"

Rick then looked out over the green meadows of the estate of Momma Bea. "The good Lord above will send her to me. I don't know when. I know she will come but real soon, I will set my eyes upon her again. She then will take the seat and full the quest of superseding the legacy of Momma Bea."

"Who is she?"

"I have seen her in a dream of mine, a life for from the reality in which we dwell." In his heart, he knew that his daughter lived somewhere in the hills of California. He knew that at any time, she would be coming back to look for her father, if she would only accept his cover-up as a woman.

He and John turned around and rode back to the house. The next morning when they got up and went to church, the spirit was really moving in Rick. He was about sixty-seven at the time and still looked good for his age. John was sixty-nine years old. While the choir was singing one of Rick's favorite songs, it really moved him to do something he had not done in a long time. He got up and walked up to the choir director and told him a song that he had on her heart. Once the church realized what it was that she was doing, they then said, "Amen." They knew that she could sing, but they had not heard her sing, at least they had not heard him sing since he was a little boy. The song he sung was "Wind Thy Will Is Done." He sung it with all his might, while the choir backs him up. While he was singing, John was sitting at the back in his office, looking over his sermon. When he heard him sing the song, the spirit moved him, so he got up out of his chair from the desk and walked out on the stage, dressed in his preacher's robe, and grabbed the other microphone from the pulpit and began singing with her—it was the most beautiful song you ever wanted to hear.

Rick was so filled with the spirit that water filled the wells of his eyes because he knew that the life in which he was living was so full of deceit and pain. While he sang, he looked into the eyes of John. At that moment, it seemed like it made the burden lighter. He did not care in the world because he was now singing to God for the many sins that haunted his soul throughout the course of his life, and he knew that God had all the answers for all his troubles. Once the song was over, John said, "My do my wife, have a beautiful voice. You could not ask for a better wife." After church, Madam Colleen's secret and the idea of his daughter were wearing down on her.

"You know, child, there are a lot of things I regretted but in the midst of my troubles and hidden sins, John had been there for me through it all. I have you to know for the hidden secrets of my life. I prayed and read the holy book of God's word because I knew that with everything in himself before a man's life is over and said and done, God has the answers and the final word. When you do have anyone else to turn to, baby, you always have God because he can keep a secret, baby, and you do not have to worry about it getting out."

That next Sunday, John preached a sermon that touched Rick's soul to the point that he said to his very soul that he had enough. He cannot continue to live his life like this. That sermon helped him to see how the inner man of his soul was not complete with the will of God. It had hit him right in the middle of his chest. The words of Momma Mamie began to rock through his soul like that of a sword, cutting like that of a great knife in battle, telling him over and over again to get himself right with God and find out what it is that God has set for his soul. At that point, Rick did not know what it was that God wanted for his life. He became upset and walked out on John's sermon to go to the restroom, for some relief. To his surprise, he found a sixteen-year-old girl inside the restroom crying her heart out with bruises around her neck, like someone had choked her.

Madam Colleen said, "Child, what's' wrong?" Once he saw the marks on the side of her neck, he said, "Oh my god, child, how did this happen?"

The little girl said, "It was Deacon Fry. He done this to me."

"That oh son of a bitch."

"Madam Colleen, please do not tell anyone please. I am very scared." She then began to cry even more.

Anger has risen inside Rick because he thought back to the time when he was raped by his mother's boyfriend. He then hugged the child. "Hush, child, hush, child. How long have he been doing this to you?"

The girl said, "I do not know, about four or five month now."

"Oh my god, child."

"He has been doing this to me every Sunday. Will look at me across the church and tell me to go to the restroom. He would also have his wife, Mrs. Fry, to ask my mother to let me come over to clean up their house. He would take me down inside the attic and have his way with me. He said if I told anyone, they would think that I was lying, and he would come and kill me."

"I promise you, child, that no good soon of a bitch will never touch you again. You hear me, child?" Rick hugged her even closer.

Once church was over, while she and John was standing at the back doors of the church, shaking the church member's hands, Deacon Fry came up to them and tried to shake Rick's hand. He jerk his hand back from his hand and rolled his eyes at him. John shook his hand and noticed that his wife was very upset about something but did not know what. John asked Rick, "Is everything okay, Madam Colleen?"

He said, "No, I will tell you all about when we get home."

John did not say anything else; he continued to shake the members of the church as they exited the building. Once Rick and John got to the house, Rick was steamed. He took off his lack beautiful back Sunday hat and laid it on a chair inside the living quarters. John followed inside, behind her, to listen to what it was that she had to say.

John asked her, "What is it, Madam Colleen?"

He said, "That no good Deacon Fry must be stopped."

"What did he do?"

"He has been forcing sex on one of our church member little girl April, the Anderson daughter.

"Oh my god, Colleen, how do you know this to be true?"

"While you were preaching this morning, I decided to get up and go to the restroom in the back of the church. While I was washing my hands and looking in the mirror, I heard someone crying inside the restroom stall. I walked over to the tool and open the door and found her side on the side of the toilet, cry with bruises on the side of her neck. I asked the child what was wrong with her. She said that Deacon Fry had rape her. Not only that, he has been doing this for about four months now, not only at the church. He would have his wife have her come over to their house to clean up for them. When she come over, he would take her down to the attic and have his way with. I asked her why haven't she told anyone. She said that she was afraid to tell anyone because that no good man told her if she did, no one would believe her, and that he would and everyone would see how big of a hoe she was."

John said, "Do her parents know?"

"I do not know. Me you are going to have a talk with him tomorrow when he come to that church build tomorrow morning, and if he have any guilt in his eyes, I want you to whip his ass and band him for the church. Do you hear me? Because he will not get away with this."

"Should we contact his family about this matter?"

"No, not yet. Let's hear what it is that he have to say for his self and then when will call them and let them know."

The next morning, Rick and John were at the church, waiting for Deacon Fry to come to the church to ask him of this crime that he had done. Once he came to the church that morning, he was walking down the hall. Reverend John said unto him, "Deacon Fry, would you come to my office for a moment? I need to talk to you about important mater."

Deacon Fry walked inside the office and saw Rick sitting down with a disappointed look on his face. He then said unto Reverend John, "Reverend, what is it?"

John said, "My wife told me on yesterday that she found Sister April inside the restroom during church service, crying, and she said you had raped her."

Deacon Fry said, "That girl is lying. I know nothing of this."

Madam Colleen said, "I dare you stand here in the Lord church and lie to use to our face. Must we call her parents and the child and see what they have to say about it? You have disgrace everything this church stand for, a friend to my family and a member this for many years, and this how you do shame the church like this."

Once he heard these words, he bowed his head in shame. John then walked from behind his desk up to him and said, "My brother, is this true?"

Deacon Fry said, "Forgive me, reverend, forgiving me."

Reverend John said, "From this point, you will be remove from all your duties as treasure of this church, and your membership is no longer want at this church. We will be calling the child's mother and I will let her be the judge of your faith and I will leave it up you to tell your wife if the great sin that you have done. I give you until this afternoon to tell everything that has happen, and once you tell her, have her to call Madam Colleen. Do you hear me?" John then turned his back with a broken heart and looked out the windows of the office. "Now leave my present for I cannot stand to look at you."

Later on, April's mother came and rang Rick's doorbell. When he opened the door, she was standing there with tears in her eyes. She said unto Rick, "I did not know where I go from here."

Rick said, "On your knees and pray." She then hugged him tightly.

Rick and April pressed charges against Deacon Fry, and the police went to his house and arrested him. As Rick continued to talk to his unknown daughter in third person about the history of his life, he said, "Child, a person's soul may desire many things that is not good for it because of Rick's desires, they caused him much pain and many sleepless nights. Child, the devil will show you things that will lower you far from the will of the spirit and cause you to miss the blessings of God. You see, the blessing I thought that were blessing really wasn't blessing. They were curses from the lower beings of the earth. In overlooking his conscience, he continued living in a reality in which he loved so well rather than the reality that God had created for me."

Chapter 30

One day, John came inside the house one afternoon and said unto Rick, "Put on your finest dress because tonight, I want to take you out on the town for some dinner and to the symphony." They went out to one the nicest restaurants in New Orleans. Rick was so beautiful that night; he was dressed in one of his blue evening gowns with a blue hat that he got in Paris with the black mink stole on. John was very handsome; he had his black and white tuxedo. After dinner, they went to the theater for the grand event—the symphony. That man knew how to treat his woman out for a good time. Rick knew when he first laid eyes on this man, he knew that he would make him smile for a lifetime. John was truly the man of his dreams. The next morning was another relaxing morning for Rick and John. Rick requested for him and John to have breakfast on the lawn. It was a beautiful spring day; the table was decorated with white lining. John said unto Rick, as he was eating breakfast, "My beautiful wife, you look gorgeous this morning."

Madam Colleen said, "Why thank you. You look mighty fine yourself."

"You know, baby, I am a very lucky man because God has blessed me with you."

Madam Colleen's heart melted as if the love that she had for him renewed its self again. At that moment, his secret seemed to exist no longer. "My love for you, my darling man, is liken unto that of many waters that has sat sail for the gulf of a endless flow of water that steady flow to a unknown island of endless love, that the human heart desires to see. God has blessed me to see it in my life every time I look at you."

"Whatever do you mean, Madam Colleen?"

"The love waves of my heart will never meet its end because the love that flows from the both of our heart for each other one can never experience all of it in a lifetime."

Then they arose out of their seats and began to take a stroll; they both had aged gracefully. As John began to walk, he quoted his marriage vows, "I shall love you with all my heart."

Madam Colleen responded, "See which mean I will to."

"I shall be faithful to the love of your heart until the very hair on your head turns gray and the grave swallow my flesh body up and it turn back to the dust from which it comes from."

Madam Colleen responded, "See I shall love you for rich and poor, through sickness and health."

John then said, "For this is the will of God."

This time in life, John was seventy, and Colleen was sixty years old. From that point on, John served his last term as mayor of New Orleans, just before his health began to fail. That afternoon, John and Rick sat out on their back porch and thought about their life and love together. They also saw the goodness of it and did not say word to each other because their love was confirmed within the both them. Rick then grabbed John's hand and then pat it. He then looked at him, and he looked at him with a smile. They then looked out of the lawn into the sky at the sunset, in a daze of peace. They would take long walks around the house and view the beauty of their land.

When John retired as the mayor of New Orleans, he decided to dedicate the rest of his life to loving his wife and serving the church. His health began to fail even more in his old age. He would set and read his Bible while Madam Colleen would work in the flower bed of the garden. He knew that John was dying. Even more, Rick's conscience was pushing him to reveal his secret to him because he thought that he should not lie to the one he loves anymore. He felt he had done it long enough, and now is the right time, but fear of losing him kept the secret concealed even more. Then it finally happened. The good Lord above began to call John's name home. One day while John was at the church office, working on his Sunday sermon, Rick was at home looking through business reports. At this time, his hair was as white as snow; old age had sat in the lining of his beauty. His eyes had also grown dim. He had received a call from the church sectary saying that Reverend John had just passed out in his office, on the floor. She had called for the deacons, and they rushed him to the hospital. Rick then had Joe get the car; he then rushed him down to the hospital. Once he arrived at the hospital, he was very nervous, not knowing the nature of John's illness. Once he got inside the hospital, he walked to the nurses' station to find out information on the nature of his illness. He was so nervous; his hands were shaking because he knew John's body was old and weak. He did not know if he would survive it or not. Rick said to one of the nurses, "My name is Madam Colleen, the former major's wife. I want to know, baby, how is he doing?"

Once the doctor realized who she was and who it was that she was asking for, he walked up to the nurses' station, where she was to answer her questions. The doctor said, "Hello, my name is Dr. Gregory James."

Madam Colleen said, "How is he?"

"Your husband will be just fine. He is stabilized. He just had a light stroke. From this point on, he will have to watch what it is that he eat. I have prepared a diet for him to follow. If he follow the diet accord to plan, it will cut down on his chance of every contracting another stroke again. We will keep him for a couple weeks so that we can keep an eye him before we let him go home."

"Thank the Lord. Where is he? Can I see him?"

"Yes, you can, right this way."

Once she walked inside the room, John was asleep. She did not wake him up; she just sat in a chair beside his bed and held is hand until he awoke from the medication that the doctor gave him. Finally, in the middle of the night, he awoke and noticed that he was sitting inside, holding his hand. He said in a soft, weak voice, "I am happy to see you, Madam Colleen. This old body of mine has taken a lickin', but the Lord has allowed me to stay around for you a bit long to protect you a little while long."

Madam Colleen said with tears inside his eyes, "My love, I have thanked the good Lord above for letting you stay a little while longer with me. Now rest so I can take you home and take care of you, my love." While he rubbed his head, John fell asleep.

After two weeks of staying inside the hospital, he made a strong recovery and came home. When he and Madam Colleen arrived in the driveway, the church members walked outside the house with balloons in their hands, saying unto him, "Welcome home!"

Madam Colleen had invited a lot of the church members over to surprise him when he got home. He was very happy and surprised to know that many of his friends cared for him. From that point on, in his old age of seventy-five years, he just sat around the house and studied the Word of God and took care of the needs of the church, while on the other hand, Madam Colleen kept herself pretty busy with the Elite Women's Club and the company. One beautiful afternoon, as the sun was rising, John was sitting out on the back desk, looking out on the lawn, thinking about his life in the presence of God. Madam Colleen was inside the house taking care of her work inside her office; she then decided the join him on the back deck. Once she got outside, she took her seat beside him. John then said, "Madam, today is a beautiful day."

He then said, "Yes, my lord, it is."

"My beloved, life has been beautiful for the both of us. The Lord has blessed us and has given you unto me, and for that I am grateful."

"My lord, I am over blessed by God. He has given me you, the most precious gift a lady could every hope for even though through the many mistake I have made in this life, all I every wanted out of life was to love you even if it killed me in doing so."

John said unto the madam, "May we take a walk?"

They then walked down the steps to take a stroll through their beautiful flower garden, on their back lawn.

John stopped. "My beloved, our love has become firm by your walking one with me. Together we will share the responsibilities of the home, food, and finances. May God bless us with noble children to share. May they live long."

Madam Colleen said, "This is my commitment to you, my lord. Together we will share the responsibility of the home, food, and finances. I promise that I shall discharge all of my share of the responsibilities for the welfare of the family and the children."

"Oh, my beloved, now you have walked with me the second step, may God bless you. I will love you and you alone as my wife. I will fill your heart with strength and courage: this is my commitment and my pledge to you. May God protect the household and children."

"My lord, at all times, I shall fill your heart with courage and strength. In your happiness, I shall rejoice. May God bless you and our household."

"Oh, my beloved, now since you have walked three steps with me, our wealth and prosperity will grow. May God bless us. May we educate our children, and may they live long."

"My lord, I love you with single-minded devotion as my husband. I will treat all other men as my brothers. My devotion to you is pure, and you are my joy. This is my commitment and pledge to you."

"Oh my beloved, it is a great blessing that you have now walked four steps with me. May God bless you. You have brought auspiciousness and sacredness in my life."

"Oh, my lord, in all acts of righteousness (Dharma), in material prosperity (Artha), in every form of enjoyment, and in those divine acts such as fire sacrifice, worship and charity, I promise you that I shall participate, and I will always be with you."

"O my beloved, now you have walked five steps with me. May Mahalakshmi make us prosperous? May God bless us."

"Oh, my lord, I will share both in your joys and sorrows. Your love will make me very happy."

"Oh, my beloved goddess, by walking six steps with me, you have filled my heart with happiness. May I fill your heart with great joy and peace, time and time again. God bless you."

"My lord, may God bless you. May I fill your heart with great joy and peace. I promise that I will always be with you."

"Oh, my beloved, as you the seven steps with me, our love and friendship have become inseparable and firm. We have experienced spiritual union in God. Now you have become completely mine. I offer my total self to you. May our marriage last forever."

"My Lord, by the law of God and the holy scriptures, I have become your spouse. Whatever promises I gave you, I have spoken them with a pure heart. All the angels are witnesses to this fact. I shall never deceive you, nor will I let you down. Forever I shall love you."

After they quoted there vows unto each other, they then turned and walked back to the deck to take a seat. Both of them sat and were filled with contentment and peace inside their souls. As Madam Colleen poured the both of them a glass of cool tea, something inside him knew that the love of his life was slowly passing away from her.

Within the next couple weeks, John had another stroke. Madam heard something fell. When she heard the noise, something within her knew that there was something wrong with John. Once he made it to the top of the stairway, he rushed to the room and found John lying out on the floor. He rushed over and saw that he was unconscious and screamed out for Joe. Once Joe made it inside the room, he said, "Hurry and call the ambulance!"

On their way to the hospital, Madam Colleen was very silent, not knowing what to think, leaving it in the hands of God. His heart had been broken because he knew it would not be long before he would be taken by the mighty hands of God. He asked himself, *Could it be that the Lord getting ready to take this great man away from me? The man of whom I had sworn to love for the rest of my life?* At this point in life, he knew that he must tell him of his secret that he had kept from him from the very beginning of their relationship until now. That thing that has haunted him since the moment he laid eyes on him. Once they arrived at the hospital, the doctor was waiting on their arrival. Madam Colleen then asked him, "How is his condition?"

Once he came back from his examination, the doctor said, "He had a very bad one this time. His body is too weak to withstand it. It's just a matter of time. There is nothing else I can do for him."

Madam Colleen's heart weakened from the disturbing news. He then pulled himself together. "Can I see him?"

"Yes, you can. He just resting, right this way."

Madam Colleen walked through the doors of his room quietly. Once he entered inside and saw him lying inside the bed with his eyes closed, he knew that it would not be long before the angels of God come and take his hand. He was not worried; he knew that this man was the greatest man who ever lived, a man who was loving and respectful, and that he had found favor with God. He knew that he must tell him now or the burden would trouble her for so many years. In that way, he could repent of his great sin, and he could see him again in that great getting up morning. He then walked close to his bedside. His eyes then opened, as if he felt the presence of his love near. He said, "My darling madam, who has superseded the legacy of Momma Bea like no other madam before her. The woman of whom I have vowed to love until my existence ends."

Madam Colleen's heart melted. Upon hearing these words, tears then began fall from his eyes.

"You know, in the molding of my being, I have loved you."

"I know, baby, I know."

Holding his hand softly, John said, "I believe the time has come for me to leave you behind."

Madam Colleen began to break down like that of an old oak tree kneeling at this great man's bed of departure. "There is something I that I have to tell you for so many years. I just didn't know how to tell you."

"Everything is well with my soul." He then rubbed her hand and said, "Need not to worry yourself for the Lord has prepared a room for me to enter in."

Madam Colleen said again, "Listen to me, o man of God, there is something I need to tell you so that I may rest my head in peace when my time come. This has haunted me since our union together in marriage." He did not know how to let the secret words flow from his mouth. "I must let you know."

John then raised his finger from his bedside and placed it on her lips and said. "Shhhh, there is no need, my darling, rest your mind for the lord in heaven has heard you repentful heart, and he forgives you. Everything is well with your soul." He then smiled.

As Madam Colleen cried his heart out, John then rose up like that of a mighty man to hug him.

Madam Colleen said, "For you have truly been a friend that stick closer then a brother, like Jonathon had a love for David like you have for me." She thought himself, *Could it be that this man know of the secret of my curse that has haunted me since my youth?*

John then looked at Madam Colleen again as the angel of God began dressing him. He said, "Everything is well with my soul, friend. Everything is well with my soul." He then closed his eyes and let his hand go. He said, "No, John, don't leave me now. I need you. You good man you. Who will love me now that you are gone?"

Madam Colleen then prepared for his funeral services. It was a big funeral. They had it at the church building; all his preacher friends were there, including many city officials. There were so many people there. There were people standing outside of the church. His best friend, Ramon, preached the funeral; his favorite song "Amazing Grace" was played.

After John's death, Madam Colleen's life was lonely yet peaceful because the curse of her secret had been lifted. He no longer had to lie to the man he loved anymore, and he was at peace with God. After his death, he had a lot of work on his hands. There was no preacher to supersede him; it was now left up to him to find another man of God to fill John's shoes as preacher.

About two weeks after John's funeral, Madam Colleen called for a deacon meeting so they could choose the next preacher; however, he had already decided who would take his place—John's assistant, Corey Pittman. But he wanted to talk to the deacons first to express his idea on Monday at noon. All the deacons gathered inside her study in the mansion; they all waited patiently for her to enter into the room, where they were waiting. Joe opened the door and said, "Madam Colleen, the former First Lady of New Orleans and the former preacher's wife is ready to enter."

Everyone stood until she took her seat. Everyone took their seat, and Joe closed the door behind him. Madam Colleen said, "Good afternoon, gentleman. This is a sad occasion for all of us. The good Lord above has taken our preacher Reverend John Smith and my dear friend and husband. As you know that there is no preacher as of yet chosen to take his place as a preacher of the Mount Zion Baptist Church and is left up to us to decide who will take his place as preacher and continue preaching the unadulterated word of God. I have been thinking, and for the past couple of years, I've been listening closely to the desires of my husband's heart in regards to this day. And I am convinced that if he was here and can choose a man for the job, he would choose his assistant who has worked diligently with him over the years. He has shown a strong dedication and loyalty to Mount Zion Baptist Church, Reverend Corey Pittman. If there is anyone in this room that opposes my proposal in choosing Reverend Corey Pittman as the new preacher of Mount Zion Baptist Church, please speak now or forever hold your peace."

The whispers of voices fell among the great men of God that day then within seconds, the whispers evaporated, and silence filled the room. And then Madam Colleen said,

"Will anyone second the motion?" And then the whole room said, "I..."

And that moment, a voice rose up from among the deacons and said, "Madam Colleen, there is a question that has pondered our minds for sometime now. If you did not know, after the death of Reverend Pittman, the deeds of Mount Zion Baptist Church rest in the hands of your cousin, Rick Lee Smith, and for many years, we have not heard from him neither have we seen him, so now, we ask you this question, where is he? Whose hands shall we put the deeds of in the church in?" Then the room became silent, waiting for his response.

Madam Colleen then stood from his seat, with tears in her eyes, feeling the redemption of God running through her veins and said, "Oh, men of God, the man of whom you speak is very much whom I have known from my age of accountability. He is very much alive and well."

Then the men began talking among themselves with amazement.

Madam Colleen continued, "Let the deeds of the church continue to rest in his hands. When the good Lord above lay my head to rest, then the deeds of the church shall rest in the hands of the next madam Elaine Smith, Rick Lee Smith's daughter."

And then the deacons of the church said, "We know nothing if this child in which you speak."

Madam Colleen said unto them, "This child has been sent to us by God."

And the men said, "It shall be done."

Madam Colleen continued to speak to his unknown daughter on the back part of the mansion. "Because of my state, I am dressed and I look like that of a woman, even though I have changed my mind from doing those sins that went against God, the only question that lies in the back of my mind that has not been answered by God himself: Will God accept me in my old age for my outward appearance even though my mind has been brought into subjection to do his will?"

Elaine pondered the question and then asked him, "What are you trying to tell me, Aunt Colleen?"

Rick then said unto her, with tears filling the wells of aged eyes, "Baby honey child, I am Rick Lee Smith, your father."

Elaine began to cry with amazement, and shock ran through her body. She was speechless. As both of them stood to hug each other, Madam Colleen then asked her, "Tell me something, Madam Elaine, my long lost daughter, will you give me a madam that will supersede the legacy of Momma Bea?"

Elaine then said, sniffling, "Yes, father, I will give you a madam that will supersede the legacy of Momma Bea."

At that moment, the Zulu witch slave walked across the porch, stared Rick in the eye, and then she vanished.

Rick began to laugh just like all the madam did before him when they asked the little madam this same question.

Bibliography

Daiker, Donald A., Mary Fuller, and Jack E. Wallace. *Literature Option For and Writing Second Edition*, 1989.

Drayton, Michael. *Since There's No Help*. 1619.

Frost, Robert. "Devotion." http://poetry.poetryx.com/poem /1931/.

Hugh, Langston. "I Am the Darker Bother." www.poemhurt.com/poem/i-too.

"Matrimonial India Wedding Customs Hindu Marriage Vows." http://www.indianslivingdbroad.com.

Shakespeare, William. "Shall I Compare Thee to a Summer's Day." 1609.